# THE SPANISH HOUSE

For Lynn Forster, the restoration of paintings had always been a peaceful living — until she went to the home of aristocratic wine-importer Brett Sackville. Lynn couldn't keep from falling in love with this arrogant man. Then she met his half-brother, Rafael. Brett refused to believe she felt nothing for Rafael, and Lynn knew that the cruel game Brett made her play to protect Rafael's heart could end only by breaking hers.

*Books by Nancy John
in the Linford Romance Library:*

LOOKALIKE LOVE

NANCY JOHN

# THE SPANISH HOUSE

*Complete and Unabridged*

# LINFORD
*Leicester*

First published in the
United States of America

First Linford Edition
published 1997

British Library CIP Data

John, Nancy, *1924*–
    The Spanish house.—Large print ed.—
    Linford romance library
    1. English fiction—20th century
    2. Large type books
    I. Title
    823.9'14 [F]

    ISBN 0–7089–5016–7

Published by
F. A. Thorpe (Publishing) Ltd.
Anstey, Leicestershire
Set by Words & Graphics Ltd.
Anstey, Leicestershire
Printed and bound in Great Britain by
T. J. Press (Padstow) Ltd., Padstow, Cornwall

This book is printed on acid-free paper

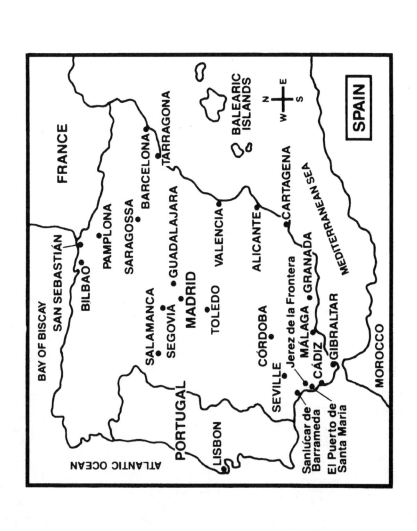

# 1

IN the maze of narrow, steep-banked Sussex lanes Lynn found the big Rover difficult to manoeuvre. For the umpteenth time she decided that she really must trade it in for a smaller car, but it would be a wrench to part with something that had been so dear to her father's heart. Anyway, she thought with a stab of despondency, hadn't she better wait to see how things were going before making any hasty decisions? She might not be able to afford to run a car at all.

At the next intersection there were five roads to choose from, and not a signpost in sight. She was lost, she might as well admit it! Perhaps, back at that last farmhouse, she should have turned left instead of right.

Beyond the hedge a tractor engine roared into life. Lynn jumped out of the car and scrambled up the high bank, frothy with cow parsley and starred with pink campion, until she could see over the hedge into the field. The tractor was driven by a swarthy young man, and hauled a truck in which a second young man of similar appearance lounged contentedly. Both were stripped to the waist, their torsos burnt nut-brown by the sun.

Lynn waved to attract their attention and the tractor changed course, veering towards her. When it was only a few yards away the driver cut the engine, and she heard him ask his companion, "Is she real, Steve, or am I dreaming?"

Two pairs of appreciative eyes surveyed the attractive girl whose upper half appeared to be sprouting from the quickthorn hedge like Venus arising from the waves. They took in Lynn's silken mass of honey-gold hair, her lustrous amber eyes, the perfect oval of her face, and her slender, softly-moulded figure, of which the blue-and-white striped shirt revealed no more than an enticing hint.

"She couldn't be real!" Steve opined. "We both suffer from overactive imaginations, Bill, that's the explanation. If we blink, I reckon she'll vanish into thin air."

"All right, you've had your fun," said Lynn crisply. "Now please can you tell me which road to take for a house called *La Casa Española*?"

"You're going to The Spanish House?" queried the driver, and let out a long, heartfelt sigh of envy. "Some men have all the luck! Still, with his money and his looks, it's no wonder he can get the girls!" He gave Lynn a grin that was impudently admiring. "Take the right-hand lane, love, and after you've crossed the river by the old stone bridge you'll see a pair of white gates on your left."

"Thanks a lot!"

Lynn almost fell down the bank in her eagerness to escape from those appraising eyes. As she drove on, her

3

mind was busy considering the none-too-subtle hints the men had dropped about the owner of *La Casa Española*. It rather sounded as if Brett Sackville was unmarried. If so, she hoped with a tiny shiver of apprehension that he was not living alone at the house. Such a situation would be fraught with embarrassing possibilities if, as she anticipated, she'd be staying there for a while.

She crossed the hump-backed bridge, manoeuvred the car between newly-painted white gates and drew up before a long, low house which, unsurprisingly, was built in the Spanish style. A white facade, gleaming in the bright sunshine, was topped by a tiled roof of warm orange-brown, and running along two sides of the building was a wide patio with pillars linked by semi-circular arches. The grounds appeared to be extensive, with numerous trees, among which cypresses featured largely, along with flower beds vibrant with the colours

4

of early summer, and neatly-tended lawns.

Very nice, too, for those who could afford it, Lynn thought appreciatively, as she took her suitcase from the trunk and carried it over to the glazed front door. Her ring was answered almost at once and, much to her relief, by a pleasant-looking middle-aged woman. Her figure was comfortable without being actually plump, and she was quietly dressed in dark green, her greying hair drawn back in a bun. There was the soft lilt of the Scottish highlands in her voice as she addressed Lynn.

"Good afternoon to you." Her glance travelled speculatively to the suitcase. "And who might you be, young lady?"

"I'm Lynn Forster. Mr. Sackville asked me to come about the paintings."

"I see!" The guarded smile at once grew more welcoming, the door swung open wider. "Come you in, my dear! Leave your case there . . . it's heavy for you to carry upstairs, and my husband will fetch it in just a minute. If you'll kindly follow me, I'll show you to the room I've prepared." Turning to the stairs, she glanced back at Lynn apologetically. "It was a gentleman I was expecting, you ken. It just never occurred to me that an art restorer might be a young lady. I hope you won't find the room too spartan for you, but men do so object to the little feminine fripperies."

"I'm sure it will suit me very nicely," Lynn smiled.

This was amply confirmed a few moments later when Mrs. Mackenzie, as the housekeeper introduced herself, showed Lynn into the bright, spacious bedroom. Decorated in cool dove-grey and white, it was close-carpeted and curtained in shades of rich magenta. Impulsively, Lynn crossed to the window, which was open wide to the balmy afternoon air, and gazed out beyond the beech hedge bordering the grounds, across green meadows where sheep and cattle grazed, to the soft, tree-flanked slopes of the South Downs. A scene of beauty and utter tranquility — what a contrast to the hectic noise and bustle of London!

"I don't know how long I shall be staying," she explained to Mrs. Mackenzie. "I've simply agreed to come and look at the oil paintings which need renovating, and give my opinion on what can be done. If it's a straightforward job I shall be able to work on them here, but they might have to be taken away."

The housekeeper nodded. "Mr. Sackville asked me to tell you that he'll be here for dinner tomorrow, and you can tell him then what you've decided." Her glance measured Lynn approvingly. "I hope you'll be staying a wee while, Miss Forster, for I do so enjoy having someone to look after."

"Doesn't Mr. Sackville spend much time here?" Lynn queried.

"Och, he comes and goes! He has a wee flat in London, and then he's frequently off to Spain." Her grey eyes misted with sadness. "Aye, it's quiet here these days . . . not like it was when Mr. Sackville's father was alive and they all lived here, with the young master a real rascal and into every sort of mischief he could think of!" She sighed. "*La Casa Española* is rightly a family home. It's no' the place for a man on his own!"

"You didn't mention Mr. Sackville's mother," said Lynn. "Is she dead, too?"

"Bless you no, though I fear her health isn't all it might be. She married again, and has been widowed a second time, poor lady. She wed one of the Spanish side of the business — they're all in wine, you know — and her home is on the family estate out there now. She's Señora Victoria Alejandro these days, and the son she had by her second husband is as different from his half-brother as chalk is from cheese."

The housekeeper might have continued, but there was a tap on the door and a plumpish, mild-faced man with grey hair entered, carrying Lynn's suitcase. As he put it down, he nodded to her with a friendly grin.

"This is Miss Forster, Dougal, who's come to do the paintings," his wife introduced them. And to Lynn she added, "If you'll give my husband your keys, he'll run your car into the garage for you."

"Thanks!" Lynn fished in her handbag. "And would you mind bringing in the things from the trunk . . . my box of equipment and my easel."

"With pleasure, miss!" he said, and departed.

Mrs. Mackenzie too went to the door. "Now I'll leave you to freshen up, Miss Forster, while I get you some tea. Just give a wee shout if you need anything."

Alone, Lynn kicked off her shoes and enjoyed the feel of the thick, velvety carpet between her toes. A second door, standing ajar, led to a well-fitted bathroom, replete with sufficient soft fluffy towels for three

9

people, let alone one! The London flat she'd shared with her father and which she still occupied (though she knew she couldn't afford the rent for much longer), was comfortable in a rambling Victorian way, but this was real luxury! Lynn sighed contentedly, promising herself a gloriously long soak in the huge bathtub this evening. Meanwhile she quickly washed at the sink, changed her dress, and went downstairs.

She was served tea at a little round table on the patio, and enjoyed the aromatic delicacy of the Earl Grey blend, the wafer-thin cucumber sandwiches, sultana scones, and — indulging herself just for once — a cream-filled chocolate eclair. Afterwards, she got straight down to work.

The four paintings requiring attention were all in the study, a room with a strong aura of masculinity, panelled in oak, with bookshelves lining the whole of one wall. The pictures, Lynn judged, were the work of an early nineteenth-century artist, horse paintings somewhat in the style of George Stubbs. Rather nice, she decided.

A mahogany library-table by the window offered the best light, and before starting her examination Lynn cleared its surface of various small objects. About to put aside a gilt-framed photograph, she paused and studied it. It showed an elegant, silver-haired lady reclining in a basket chair beneath a blossom tree. Behind her stood a tall, much younger man, with dark, almost black hair and deeply penetrating eyes . . . eyes that seemed to be looking out of the photograph directly at Lynn, giving her the uneasy sensation of being observed . . . and found wanting! On the back of the photo was written in a bold, forceful hand, *Taken at Los Pámpanos*, and then a date from the previous summer. The lady would be Señora Alejandro, Lynn surmised. And was the man her elder or her younger son? Her elder son, by her first marriage, presumably, as the inscription was in English. Anyway, she would know tomorrow, when Brett Sackville came to hear her verdict on his paintings.

Applying herself to her task, Lynn examined the pictures one by one and was relieved to find that the job of restoration was well within her capabilities. The main problem seemed to be the familiar one of bloom — the old natural-resin types of varnish were the cause of so much trouble! Opening her box of equipment, she selected a bottle of white spirit and moistened a wad of cotton wool, with which she wiped a small area of canvas. This confirmed her opinion that the painting beneath the varnish was in relatively good condition.

After doing a few further tests, Lynn decided to call it a day. She went outside and strolled around the grounds, noting the well-kept grass tennis court enclosed by a clipped yew hedge, and the oval-shaped swimming pool hidden away behind a sentry-line of cypress trees. At the end of the gardens, she climbed a stile leading into a grove of oak saplings, their tender new leaves gently unfurling. It was all so beautiful, Lynn thought with a sigh, and wished she was more knowledgeable about things like wild flowers and birds.

The chill of the evening air on her bare arms sent her back to the house for supper, an attractively-served meal of grilled sole and orange mousse, with a glass of chilled white wine as an accompaniment. After coffee, Lynn retired early to her room, intending to read for an hour in bed before settling down to sleep.

But instead, she lay back enjoying the feeling of unobtrusive luxury . . . the wide bed, the crisp sheets and the warm radiance of the silk-shaded bedside light. A complete hush seemed to envelop the countryside until she became aware of small, soft sounds . . . the sleepy murmuring of birds, the whisper of leaves, and, from far off in the woods, the scarcely detectable bark of a fox.

The worries that had pursued her these past weeks seemed suddenly to have evaporated. Her problems, unaccountably, were problems no more. When the telephone call from Brett Sackville's secretary had come the other day, Lynn had been at the end of her tether, acknowledging bleakly that it was hopeless to try and carry on the art restoration business built up by her father. The two of them had been close, thrown together by the tragically early death of Lynn's mother. From the age of fifteen, Lynn had looked after her father's home, and thanks to an inherited artistic flair, she had rapidly assimilated a lot of his professional skill. But now that her father was dead, she couldn't expect to cope with the more intricate repairing and restoring work for which Charles Forster had been justly famed.

This job at *La Casa Española* was comparatively simple and right up Lynn's alley, but how was she going to ensure a steady supply of such commissions? Better to give up gracefully, her prudence advised, and find a job in an office. But that was a step Lynn was loath to take, for it would seem like letting her father down.

If Mr. Sackville agreed to her recommendations, she would have work here for two or three weeks at most. After that, what? Lynn knew she should feel concern about the future, but somehow she couldn't. Lying there in these luxurious surroundings, she felt a glow of optimism steal over her and soon she drifted into an untroubled slumber.

Lynn's happy mood persisted into the morning, which heralded yet another of the hot, sunny days of this early summer heatwave. After breakfast, Lynn wrote up her notes on the paintings, detailing the work needing to be done and giving a rough estimate of the cost. This was an unbroken rule established by her father to avoid the chance of any misunderstanding.

By noon she was finished. Luncheon was at one-thirty, Mrs. Mackenzie had told her, and the thought of the cool, sapphire-blue water of the swimming pool was enticing.

"Would it be possible for me to use the pool?" she asked tentatively.

"Indeed, yes! My Dougal keeps the filtration plant going and skims the leaves every day, but as often as not it's never used from one weekend to the next. I'll bring your lunch to the poolside if you like . . . it's just cold ham and salad. You'll be having a cooked meal with Mr. Sackville when he arrives this evening."

Lynn ran up to her room and fetched her bikini . . . two minuscule wisps of canary-yellow nylon. There was a chalet to change in, and when she emerged she found that Dougal had been despatched to set up a long lounge chair for her, with an elegant white ironwork table beside it. Deciding to sunbathe before her swim, Lynn lay back in the lounge chair and gratefully closed her eyes, enjoying the blissful warmth on her bare skin.

The minutes slipped by and Lynn dozed, lulled by the distant sound of a farm tractor ... perhaps the same one she had stopped yesterday to ask for directions, manned by the two husky young men who had clearly misconstrued her role at The Spanish House.

It seemed that the owner of *La Casa Española* had quite a reputation where women were concerned, and Lynn matched that image against the tall dark man in the photograph, whom she felt certain must be Brett Sackville. He had looked arrogant and self-assured, no doubt supremely confident of his power to conquer any woman who took his fancy. Well, she thought drowsily as tentacles of sleep invaded her brain, I'm only here to do a job of work, so he'd better not get any funny ideas about *me* . . .

Footsteps on the smooth paving surrounding the pool did nothing to disturb her dreams, but a man's voice shattered her into instant wakefulness. It was harsh, rude, overbearing.

"Who the devil are you?" it demanded, "And what are you doing using my pool?"

Startled, Lynn opened her eyes and was immediately dazzled by the full brilliance of the sun. The man who had spoken stood scarcely a yard away, immensely tall as he towered over her, a menacing silhouette against the brightness of the sky. Hastily, she scrambled to her feet, and stammered. "You must be Mr. Sackville. I'm Lynn Forster . . . Charles Forster's daughter."

"I see! So he's brought you with him," he said, and added witheringly, "He might have had the courtesy to ask my permission."

Lynn flinched in dismay. "No . . . you've got it all wrong! My father is dead, Mr. Sackville. I . . . I've

18

come to do the work on your paintings myself."

"You?" He looked incredulous. "But you're a girl!"

As his gaze swept over her body, emphasizing his point, Lynn wished to heaven that he hadn't caught her in such an acutely embarrassing situation — or at least, that she'd been sunbathing in something less revealing. The thought of the few square inches of yellow nylon standing between her and complete nakedness brought the colour rushing to her cheeks. She hadn't even bothered to bring her towel out from the chalet so, in a desperate attempt to take refuge from those callously appraising eyes, she donned the only thing she had handy — a pair of large round sunglasses.

"What . . . what's wrong with being a girl?" she challenged, vainly trying to keep her end up.

"Nothing. Nothing at all, Miss Forster! In appropriate situations I'm all for them! But I should be interested to know why it wasn't explained to my secretary when she phoned that you would be coming in your father's place."

"Because the question didn't arise," Lynn retorted. "Your secretary asked if she was speaking to the firm of Charles Forster, and when I confirmed that, she said would we please come and give an opinion on the possibility of restoring some paintings at your Sussex home."

"My secretary obviously expected — just as I did — that Charles Forster would be coming himself."

"Well, she didn't make that clear," Lynn flashed. Then realising that she was probably stirring up trouble for his poor secretary, she added contritely, "I'm sorry, Mr. Sackville, perhaps I should have explained the position."

He nodded, not unbending a fraction, and his voice remained curt and scathing. "And what makes you think you can do the work, Miss Forster?"

"Because I've been trained to do it by my father," she replied steadily.

"I've already examined the paintings, and there's nothing complicated about the job. I've written up notes for you of what needs to be done."

"Very well, I'll study them later," he clipped. "Meanwhile, you are at liberty to continue your sunbathing."

Disconsolately, Lynn watched him stride towards the house, tall and leanly immaculate in a dark city suit. Before Brett Sackville's arrival she'd been steeling herself against the likely advances of a philanderer. It was rather disconcerting, (to say the least), to find that his only response to her femininity was withering scorn at the idea that she could possibly possess a skill which he regarded as a strictly masculine prerogative.

The sun was still shining as warmly as ever in the clear, bright sky, but suddenly Lynn imagined a chill in the air. She felt an urgent need to get into some protective layers of clothing again. Darn this wretched bikini, she thought angrily. She doubted if she would ever be able to wear the thing again, because if she did, she would always recall those hard, relentless eyes raking over her body and making her flush with embarrassment. Anyway, she wondered defiantly, why on earth had Brett Sackville come straight to the pool on his arrival, and not gone into the house first like any normal person would have done?

She learnt the answer to that question when she met Mrs. Mackenzie in the hall a few minutes later.

"I gather from Mr. Brett that he's met you already," the housekeeper said, with a shrewdly amused glance at Lynn. "It seems that things at his office were slack for once, and he thought he might as well come down here early. There'd been traffic jams all the way out of London, and he'd been thinking longingly of a dip in the pool the moment he arrived."

Lynn gasped in dismay. "And my being there prevented him?"

"I don't see why that should have

stopped him, lassie. I'd have thought a pretty girl would have been an added attraction. And so would *he*, normally," she mused.

But Brett Sackville doesn't think of me as a pretty girl, Lynn sighed inwardly. To his mind I'm just a female upstart who dares to think she's an art expert. Well, I'll darn well show Mr. Brett Sackville how mistaken he is!

The pleasant *al fresco* lunch she'd been promised was now abandoned for a more formal meal taken in the dining-room with Brett Sackville. Determined that from now on the image she presented should be exactly right, Lynn had gone to her room and changed again into a white blouse and navy skirt, brisk and efficient-looking, with her honey-gold hair, which normally hung free to her shoulders, restrained by a neat velvet bandeau.

Brett Sackville, too, had changed his clothes. He now wore fawn linen slacks and a crisp blue cotton shirt, open at the neck to show the strong brown

column of his throat and the golden
gleam of a medallion that hung amid
the dark hairs of his chest. As he
offered her a glass of sherry, Lynn
decided that his mood had marginally
improved.

"I'm sorry if I stopped you having a
swim," she said awkwardly.

"Not at all!" he replied, his tone
implying that her presence would never
prevent him doing anything he might
wish to do. His dark eyes surveyed
her searchingly. "So, Miss. Forster,
you think you can handle the work
on my paintings?"

"I know I can!" she corrected. "I've
brought my notes for you to see, Mr.
Sackville."

Dismissively, he waved aside the
pages she held out to him. "I'm well
aware that my pictures aren't of great
intrinsic value, but they've been in my
family for several generations, and I
would hate to have them come to any
harm."

Lynn stemmed the angry retort that

sprang to her lips by taking a sip from her glass. "You need have no fears on that score," she said at length. "I can carry out the necessary work right here on the premises, so the paintings need never leave your house."

"You sound very confident."

"Because I know what I'm talking about," she rejoined crisply. But, if he only knew it, she was inwardly shaking before the quelling gaze of those dark eyes as he slowly drank his sherry.

At long last, so it seemed, he put the glass down and nodded his head. "Very well, Miss. Forster, you may go ahead. Will the work take long?"

"About two or three weeks, I estimate. But . . . I mean, surely you can't just decide without knowing all the details?"

His face was expressionless. "I am employing you to worry about the details. However, if you have doubts . . . "

"I haven't any doubts," she interjected.

"Very well, then!" He gestured

towards the polished mahogany dining-table, set for two. "Let us eat!"

The tender slices of ham with crisp green salad, the crusty home-baked wholewheat bread and rich farm butter, were all delicious. But Lynn couldn't enjoy her food. She was far too conscious of the man who sat across the table from her, studying her remorselessly. And his conversation was no less than a catechism.

"When did you lose your father, Miss. Forster?"

"About two months ago. It was very sudden."

"I'm sorry," he murmured with conventional sympathy. "Is your mother still alive?"

"No, she died when I was only fifteen."

"You have brothers and sisters, I expect?"

"No, I'm rather short of relatives. I have some second cousins who live in Scotland, and an aunt in Canada."

"But otherwise you are alone in the

world? Do you not find that rather daunting? You must be concerned about your future."

"No more than everyone else is," she replied lightly, adding with a jauntiness she certainly didn't feel, "I imagine that even successful businessmen have their private worries to contend with."

He frowned, and she could see he didn't appreciate having the tables turned on him. But at least, Lynn was relieved to note, it caused him to drop the subject of her personal life and revert to the work she was here to do.

"You might as well start right away," he said. "Which room will you use?"

"Well, I always prefer to work in natural light if possible, and I noticed you have a garden room at the back of the house with windows on three sides. I've brought all the equipment I need in the car with me, so if I could just have a table put in the room that would be fine. Does that suit you?"

"Of course! Just tell Mac what you

require in the way of a table, and he'll see to it."

"Mr. Mackenzie?"

"That's right!" The frown was back, the dark eyes critical again. "I noticed your car in the garage! It seems very large for a girl to drive."

Lynn was on the point of explaining that the Rover had been her father's special joy, and that she didn't want to part with it unless she was obliged to. But something prevented her. After all, what business was it of Brett Sackville's what car she chose to drive?

"As far as I'm aware," she said sweetly, "there's no actual law against a female possessing anything larger than a mini!"

Even as she felt a little glow of victory, Lynn had an uncomfortable suspicion that any triumph over Brett Sackville, however tiny, was hazardous and liable to come back at her like a boomerang.

That afternoon, with Dougal Mackenzie's willing help, Lynn arranged the garden room to her satisfaction and got down to work. The first few days would have to be spent in making some minor repairs such as re-attaching a few loose flakes of paint, before she could safely proceed with the devarnishing. When at last the fading daylight obliged her to pack up for the day, she felt tired but content with her progress.

Lynn cleaned her fingers with a turpentine-soaked rag, then went through to the kitchen to find Mrs. Mackenzie, in order to ask her what time dinner would be served.

"Seven-thirty is when Mr. Brett always likes to have it," the housekeeper told her, "if that's all right with you, dear?"

"Yes, of course. Naturally I'll fit in with whatever Mr. Sackville wants."

"Fine! Mind you," Mrs. Mackenzie went on ruminatively, "I'm not saying it mightn't be a good thing for him to come up against a bit of opposition in a female once in a while. Sometimes I think he has things a mite too much his own way . . . in that department at least," she added mysteriously, and disappeared into the larder.

From the kitchen, Lynn used the back staircase. At the top, a corridor on her right led to what she guessed to be the Mackenzies' quarters, and ahead of her was the main landing. Because she was seeing the layout from the opposite viewpoint, perhaps it wasn't surprising that she went to the wrong door.

Lynn was already inside the room before she halted in dismay. Mercifully, it was unoccupied, but it was at once apparent that this was Brett Sackville's bedroom. Decorated in muted greys and greens, it was a mirror image of her own room next door, its perfection marred by signs of impatient masculine occupation. His briefcase on the chest of drawers spilled some of its contents and the discarded dark city suit had been carelessly tossed onto the bed. Hesitantly, Lynn took a step forward, and noted that the label in the jacket was that of an exclusive London tailor. She put out her hand and the fine worsted cloth was smooth and soft under her fingertips . . .

A slight noise behind her made Lynn spin round in alarm to see Brett Sackville standing in the doorway, regarding her with a dark frown. But wasn't there, too, a glint of triumph in his expression, she wondered in mortification?

"I . . . I mistook the door," she stammered, feeling the colour rush to her face. "I just walked in without thinking."

"How unfortunate for you that I should appear at exactly the wrong moment," he remarked ironically. "Perhaps in future you'll make an effort to remember that your bedroom is the second door along from the head of the stairs."

"But that depends on which staircase you use," she protested. "I took the back stairs, which is how I came to make such a silly mistake."

His voice shrivelled her. "As there are three doors on this side, Miss Forster, yours is the second one whichever way you approach it."

Damn the man! she thought furiously, almost pushing past him in her haste to get away. Safely gaining her own room, she stood with her back to the door, her breast heaving, her heart pounding like a warning drumbeat.

Brett Sackville certainly had a way of getting under her skin! Was it a technique of his with women who didn't respond immediately to his undoubted sensual attraction? He might have learnt from past experience that a series of crushing verbal defeats left his victim vulnerable and easy to conquer when he finally condescended to make the attempt.

Well then, he would discover that he'd met the exception in her case, Lynn thought furiously as she dragged off her paint-spattered jeans and shirt. She was thankful it was time for a langorous bath in a deep tub of hot water, which would soak away her ruffled feelings and help to prepare her for a combative dinner engagement with Brett Sackville.

After turning on the taps, Lynn went back to the bedroom on impulse, taking the bikini from the drawer where she'd put it away earlier. For a few moments she stood there looking at the scraps of yellow fabric, then she quickly slipped out of her robe and put it on, surveying herself in the full-length mirror. Her reflection made her flush with embarrassment. Heavens, this swimsuit was even more revealing than she'd realised. Her mind went back to the episode at the pool. Brett Sackville's dark eyes raking her from head to toe, seeming to tear aside even the minimal protection the bikini offered.

Before she did any more sunbathing or swimming at *La Casa Española*, Lynn resolved, she would buy herself a more decorous one piece swimsuit. And, in future, she'd remain constantly on her guard, never giving Brett Sackville the smallest opportunity to breach her defences. She would make herself completely immune to the effect of his sardonic, sarcastic tongue.

# 2

THREE days went by, days of continuously bright May sunshine. Each morning, early, Brett Sackville set off in his big red Mercedes for his office in London. Lynn, too, made an early start, always getting to the room she'd made her studio by eight-thirty, to get the best of the morning light. By now, she had the first of the paintings propped on her easel, and had begun stripping away the old, discoloured varnish with tiny cotton wool swabs dipped in solvent. It was a laborious process, requiring meticulous care and attention to detail. But to Lynn, as it had been to her father, it was a labour of love. The joy of seeing the original bright glowing colours emerging as the artist had intended them to was a reward in itself.

If her working days were a pleasure to Lynn, the evenings were a torment. Mrs. Mackenzie seemed astonished that her employer should return to Sussex each night from London; at most, Lynn gathered, he normally spent only the weekends here. He gave as his reason the unseasonable heatwave which was making the city unbearably stuffy.

On Friday Brett Sackville was home especially early, soon after five o'clock. He found Lynn in her studio and stood watching her in silence for a few moments. But under his searching gaze, she found it impossible to continue with her task, so she put down the swab and turned to him enquiringly.

"Did you want something, Mr. Sackville?"

He hesitated a moment. "I gather you haven't been using the pool here these last few days," he said, almost as if it was a reprehensible omission on her part. "You're perfectly free to, you know."

Trying to conceal her astonishment,

Lynn replied politely, "Thank you, Mr. Sackville. I'll remember that."

He made no move to leave, wandering over to the table and carefully examining one of the pictures that Lynn had laid there after its first surface cleaning. But he made no comment on Lynn's progress.

"I'm going to have a swim myself now," he said. "Perhaps you'd care to join me."

Lynn's thoughts flew upstairs to the revealing yellow bikini hidden in one of her drawers. She blushed at the memory, and said firmly, "Thanks, but I can't really afford the time. I have to take advantage of the daylight."

"But you've been at work since early morning, Mrs. Mac tells me, with only a short break at lunchtime. Come on, a swim before dinner will freshen you up."

It almost amounted to an order, Lynn thought with a sinking heart, and since he was paying for her time here it was virtually impossible for her to refuse. How she regretted not having taken an hour off to drive into the nearby town and buy another swimsuit!

Brett Sackville moved decisively to the door. "I expect you want to clean up first, so I'll see you at the pool in ten minutes," he said briskly as he left the room.

Not to go for a swim now, and have him come and demand the reason, would only make more of the incident, Lynn decided unhappily. Besides, she couldn't deny that the prospect of a refreshing dip in the cool, clear water was enticing on such a hot day. But a last touch of defiance made her linger for almost twenty minutes, rather than ten, while she changed out of her working clothes. When she arrived at the pool, carrying her towel and the two brief wisps of yellow nylon, she was relieved to see that he was already swimming, his dark hair gleaming wetly as he cut through the water with powerful overarm strokes. She was able to slip into the chalet unnoticed.

Or so she thought! But when she emerged she was dismayed to see him waiting for her at the side of the pool. Walking the few yards to the rim, she felt horribly exposed under the steady scrutiny of his dark eyes. She wanted to turn and run back to the sheltering chalet. Instead, in her haste to dive into the concealing water, she misjudged the angle of entry and landed on the surface with a smack that knocked her breathless.

Instantly, strong hands were supporting her. Lynn felt herself drawn to the side of the pool and pinned there against the blue tiles by the lean hardness of his body. When she had blinked the water from her eyes she found that his face was only a couple of inches from hers, and she struggled feebly to get away.

"Are you all right?" he demanded, sounding concerned. "That was a nasty smack."

"My . . . my foot slipped," Lynn lied

tremblingly. She would have liked to get out and sit down for a minute while she regained her breath, but she decided it was more prudent to remain in the water. "I'm perfectly all right, honestly. You don't need to support me."

Reluctantly, it seemed, he released his hold on her and after a few moments, satisfied that she really was all right, he swam off. Holding onto the rail, Lynn trod water until he was safely across the pool, then began to swim herself, somehow contriving to keep out of his way without being too obvious about it. After a few minutes, while his back was turned, she hastily scrambled out of the water and made an undignified dash for the cover of the changing room.

Brett Sackville was no longer in the pool when she emerged once more from the chalet. He was stretched out on a lounge chair, and Lynn noted how the brown of his lean sun-tanned body contrasted with the royal blue and white of his well-cut swim trunks. The angled rays of the afternoon sun made the gold medallion on his chest gleam like a flash of fire. He indicated a chair beside him and as Lynn hesitated, searching for some excuse, Dougal Mackenzie appeared from the house bearing a tray of tea things.

"The wife thought you'd be glad of a cup," he observed.

"Good timing!" approved his employer. "Thanks, Mac!"

Not wanting to reject a kind gesture from the housekeeper, Lynn had perforce to join him. Compared with their first poolside encounter, she thought, the situation was reversed now: she was fully clothed and this time it was Brett Sackville who was nearly naked. So why, Lynn asked herself puzzledly, was she acutely self-conscious and ill-at-ease, while he seemed totally relaxed, lying back comfortably with his fingers linked behind his neck?

She busied herself with the teapot to

avoid any need to look in his direction. Yet she could sense, without looking, that his gaze was upon her, making her so nervous that the teapot rattled against the cups. No doubt this was all part of his softening-up technique, she thought angrily, and promised herself that she would retain her composure whatever the provocation.

He took the cup she offered with a brief nod of thanks. "What will you do when the job here is finished?" he asked her. "Is there plenty of work in your line?"

Lynn shrugged. "Enough! At least . . . "

"At least what?" he enquired, taking a spoonful of sugar.

She met the cool, dark eyes, and glanced away again hastily.

"I can't expect to live on my father's reputation," she explained uncomfortably. "I have to make a name for myself if I hope to succeed."

"And that," he ruminated, "means satisfied clients. Well, if you satisfy me, Miss Forster, I shall doubtless be able to put in a good word for your behalf here and there."

"An offer which is intended to make me throw myself at your feet in gratitude, I suppose?" she flashed sarcastically.

He made no reply to that, and when she found the silence beyond bearing, Lynn stole a look at him. To her confusion, she found he was regarding her with a look of puzzled surprise.

"Well, we won't argue about it," he said casually. "Perhaps I shall *not* be pleased with what you do to my paintings, and then the question of recommending you to my friends won't arise."

Later, back in her room, Lynn prepared herself with extreme care for her next encounter with Brett Sackville. For that was how she regarded their meetings . . . each one a strategic battle, too many of which she seemed to have lost ignominiously. In her present uncomfortable situation at *La Casa Española*, there were two essentials if she were to salvage her pride. First, without question, she was determined to present him with such high-class examples of picture restoration that he'd be forced to acknowledge her ability as a craftsman — or rather, craftswoman! Secondly, there were to be no more defeats. He must be made to realise that she was no mere puppet on a string, ready to be manipulated as his whim demanded.

Soaking luxuriously in the hot water, Lynn reflected on how strange it was that, although she had deliberately kept her gaze averted from Brett Sackville as he lounged beside her at the poolside, she could visualise every detail of him with crystal clarity . . . long legs crossed at the ankles, lean hips encased in brief swim trunks, broadening to a hard, contoured chest from which dark hairs curled damply around the gold links of his St. Christopher chain. The lines of his jaw and face were firm and incisive. His eyes — a very deep slate-grey, she decided — were widely spaced beneath the strong straight line of his brow. His hair, such a dark shade of brown that it was hard to distinguish it from black except for the rich glints it reflected, was crisp and springy and worn fairly long, curling slightly into his neck.

Lynn dragged her mind away from the contemplation of his features, and considered what she was going to wear for dinner. She felt the need to look her very best tonight, to give herself courage and confidence. There were three options among the clothes she'd brought with her . . . a midnight-blue velvet trouser suit which she'd been told by more than one admiring male made her look extremely sophisticated, a short cocktail dress of silver lurex which was perhaps a trifle too slick for the occasion, and a long dress of uncrushable crepe in a subtle swirling design of blue and white, high on the bosom and falling in softly feminine folds to the floor. Lynn's mind was made up before she climbed out of the bath. The long dress it should be!

He was in the lounge as she entered, standing at the open French windows looking out at the sunset, which was making a glorious crimson blaze of the western sky. He swung round when he heard her, and his eyes widened in appreciation. Then, swiftly, his expression hardened.

"You've made yourself look very glamorous tonight, Miss Forster," he remarked, allowing the faintest touch of irony to show in his voice. "If I had known, I could have worn a dinner jacket."

Lynn lifted her chin, and defiantly uttered a blatant untruth. "This is the coolest thing I have for a warm evening. That's the only reason I put it on."

"I see!" he said, clearly not believing her. "I must say it is very . . . effective!"

Did he really imagine she'd chosen this dress in order to captivate him, she wondered furiously. Lynn had a good mind to dash upstairs and change into something plain and ordinary, but a warning inner voice prevented her in time. To do that would be to hand him victory on a plate, she told herself.

His own attire, in fact, could not have better complemented hers if he had chosen it for the purpose. He wore a lightweight, navy suit, with an embroidered cream shirt and a silk tie the rich colour of claret. It was impossible to deny that he was a very handsome man, and she could understand that many women would find him extremely attractive.

They adjourned to the dining-room next door, and Mrs. Mackenzie served the meal . . . a cold consommé to start with, followed by grilled lamb cutlets with tender broad beans and buttered new potatoes. Lynn finished with a fluffy baked apple sweetened with honey and smothered with yellow cream, but he chose cheese and biscuits. Each meal at *La Casa Española* had been up to this standard . . . good food excellently cooked, but without undue frills. The wine, as to be expected of a wine-importer, was superb.

At first their conversation was confined to non-controversial matters like the weather and the Maytime appearance of the countryside. Then, out of the blue, he asked her, "Are you planning on staying here right through the weekend?"

This was what Lynn *had* been planning, intending to work through Saturday and take Sunday off to see something of the surrounding district. But with a feeling of dismay she wondered if she'd been taking too much for granted. Did he want her out of the way?

"I . . . I could go back to London, if you'd prefer it, and return on Monday morning," she faltered.

He shook his head with a trace of impatience. "You're perfectly welcome to remain here, Miss Forster, if you wish. I merely thought you'd probably have some weekend engagements."

"No, I . . . I've nothing fixed."

He reached across and refilled her wineglass.

"Your fiancé must be an exceedingly . . . patient man, to agree to be parted from you for so long."

"What made you think I have a fiancé?" she parried, after a little pause. "I'm not wearing an engagement ring."

"True!" he acknowledged. "I used the term loosely. No doubt there is someone with whom you have an, er . . . understanding?"

She gave a small shake of the head. "Not really!"

"You amaze me! You have the sort of looks that would undermine a man's resistance. I cannot believe that you have never received a proposal of marriage."

Lynn hesitated. Taken at face value, she supposed, his words could be construed as a compliment — but not his manner of saying them! As always with him, there was an undercurrent of derision, of mockery. She forced herself to reply steadily, removing any trace of anger from her voice.

"Yes, Mr. Sackville, I *have* received a proposal of marriage."

"And you refused it?"

"Obviously I did, since I am neither married nor engaged!"

"And might I enquire who this suitor was, who failed to measure up to your requirements? An ineffectual character, perhaps, who hadn't advanced to a position of sufficient standing in the world?"

"On the contrary," she flashed back. "Roger Hardwick was a man of considerable strength of character and integrity. He was an executive for a shipping line, and when his firm asked him to take charge of their Montreal office, he wanted me to go to Canada with him as his wife."

Brett Sackville looked impressed. "A tempting prospect! I wonder why you refused him."

"For the best of reasons," she replied crisply. "I didn't accept Roger's proposal because I didn't love him. I respected him . . . I was very fond of him, and I believe that he sincerely loved me. But I found I just couldn't reciprocate his feelings."

"You're ambitious, Miss Forster, I'll say that for you! To turn down a business executive, no doubt highly paid, in the confident expectation of finding someone even better!"

"You make marriage sound like some sordid commercial bargain," she flared angrily.

"Isn't that exactly what it is in the majority of cases? I seem to remember a phrase 'the marriage market' which aptly describes the situation."

"What a very cynical view you take of life," she retorted.

"Of women!" he corrected. "Members of your sex, Miss Forster, are very ready to talk of 'being in love' if a man's bank balance is large enough."

"If you seriously believe that, Mr. Sackville, you have little experience of my sex."

Lynn could have bitten off her tongue

the moment the words were uttered. She heard — as she was meant to hear — the derision in his voice.

"I fear I must correct you there, Miss Forster. I have had considerable experience of your sex. That's what has led me to the conclusion you refer to as so 'cynical.'"

Lynn had difficulty in controlling her breathing as she said quietly, "Then you must have made some unfortunate choices, that's all I can say. Naturally, I'm not denying there are a few women like that."

"Believe me, there are more than a few! From my viewpoint, the world seems populated with scheming females who see me as nothing more than a free passport to a life of comfort and idleness."

"If you think you understand women so well," she rejoined, "then why waste your time on them?"

His eyes widened with satisfaction at having trapped her into giving him another opening.

"Did I say I wasted my time on them? You have my word for it, Miss Forster, that the hours I've spent with some of those young ladies have been put to excellent use. But not, I admit, with quite the 'happy ending' they had been hoping for. I remain free and unfettered . . . unscathed, one might say!"

"And lonely!" Lynn rapped back at him before she could stop herself.

He gave her a puzzled glance. "Why do you say that?"

Lynn's throat was parched and she longed to take a sip of the cool white wine before her. But she dared not lift her glass, for her trembling hand would betray her.

"Sadly, everyone isn't lucky enough to find true love," she said in a quiet voice, realising, even as she spoke, how self-confidently young she must sound. "But we must all *aim* to find it, one day, and we go on hoping, never giving up. To reject every member of the opposite sex as an insincere schemer is . . . is a policy of despair! If you cannot visualise ever giving yourself to another person in complete trust and confidence, there seems little point in going on living."

There was a lengthy silence between them. A faint evening breeze blew in through the open windows, riffling the curtains and tinkling the crystal pendants of the chandelier suspended above the table.

"You speak very forcefully," he said at last, pushing back his chair and rising to his feet. "Almost as if you really believe what you've just said."

"I do!" she replied, also rising. "I was never more convinced of anything in my life."

"You may find your idealistic theories put to a severe test," he suggested, with a thin, mirthless smile. "Perhaps you'll discover that you're ready after all to settle for something far short of the perfect love you claim to hold so dear."

"I doubt that," Lynn countered

shakily, hoping that her nervousness was not apparent to him.

"We shall see!" he commented. "In due course, we shall see!"

Usually, after dinner, Brett withdrew to his study while Lynn returned to the lounge to watch television on the large colour set, or read a book. This evening, to her astonishment, he came with her to the lounge. The housekeeper, too, was clearly caught by surprise, arriving with the coffee things on two separate trays. She put both down on the low table beside Lynn, giving her a secret look in which raised eyebrows featured largely.

When the two of them were alone again, he asked if she would care for a liqueur with her coffee.

"Thank you, a very small one." Not to appear ignorant, she named the only liqueur she'd so far tasted. "Have you some cherry brandy?"

"Certainly!" He reached into the buffet cupboard and extracted a bottle, pouring the syrupy red liquid into a tiny glass. "I'll join you with a cognac."

Lynn had chosen a chair to one side of the wide hearth, where a display of white lilac fragrantly scented the room. Brett took his glass and stood by the open French windows, gazing out into the darkening garden. But presently he turned and crossed to the record player, taking considerable care in making his choice from the large collection of records in the cabinet.

The music began and Lynn recognised it at once from the opening chords on the piano . . . Rachmaninov's second concerto. She wasn't particularly knowledgeable about classical music but she had her favourite pieces, and this one was at the very top of her list. It was as if, she thought wryly, Brett Sackville had an uncanny knack of matching the music to the girl. Was this one of his special accomplishments which contributed to his mastery over women and made him so arrogantly self-confident?

Steeling herself against the dangerous lyricism of the music, Lynn told herself matter-of-factly that she could surely listen to a beautiful melody without losing her head and becoming emotional. But when the second movement began, with flute and clarinet poignantly combined and the piano lending an exquisite accompaniment, she found herself filled with a strange, elusive yearning. To her chagrin, she realised that her eyes were moist with tears. Anxious to conceal her vulnerability, she rose to her feet and walked swiftly through the French doors onto the patio.

But the music followed her, a soft throbbing pulse against the cool night air. From the darkness of the garden drifted the spicy fragrance of azaleas, the warm sweet scent of wallflowers. Beyond the cypress trees a silver moon hung poised above the smooth black outline of the Downs. The beauty of it all caught at her throat and she wanted to cry.

Lynn sensed, rather than heard, his soft footfall behind her. She stood tense and unmoving, her heart-beat underscoring the passionate outpouring of the orchestra. Fatalistically, she waited for the touch of his hands, knowing that it would come, yet the moment she felt his fingertips on her bare arms she fluttered like a startled bird. Under their firmly persuasive pressure she turned to face him, seeing him as a dark silhouette against the gilded lamplight spilling from the room.

"You are very beautiful!" he whispered softly.

Brett's arms went around her and he drew her to him, holding her pressed against his long, lean body so that she could feel his masculine warmth through the thin stuff of her dress. His lips came down on hers, gently at first then with a hard insistence, and Lynn felt a sweet tide of delight flooding through her veins. As the kiss continued, exploring, demanding, her arms slid up round his neck and her fingers wound themselves into his crisply curling hair. No man had ever before brought her to this peak of sensual awareness. Her whole body seemed to be floating through soft clouds and she had a sensation of losing herself. Strange, unknown longings were stirring deep within her, and in response to Brett's mounting passion she felt a wild, reckless urge to yield to the clamouring of her instincts.

The second movement of the concerto came to an end, and in the moments of silence Lynn snapped back to her senses. She pushed away from him in horrified dismay, tearing herself from his embrace.

"Whatever's the matter?" asked Brett in surprise.

For a moment no words would come, then through the tightness in her throat, Lynn stammered, "You . . . you mustn't . . . "

Whyever not," he demanded, "when

we are obviously attracted to one another?"

"That's not true!" she denied weakly. "I . . . I don't want you to touch me."

"No?" he said, with biting sarcasm. "Then I must say you were putting on a damned good performance. You deserve an Oscar for it! I've rarely encountered a woman who gave the impression of enjoying being kissed as much as you did just now."

"But I didn't . . . I didn't . . . "

"You want me to prove my point?" Brett asked laconically, and before Lynn could stop him he had swept her into his arms and again she was locked in a fierce embrace. His lips met hers with bruising force while his hands roamed over her, moulding her soft body to meet his hardness. It was all Lynn could do to resist and not be engulfed by the heady bliss that was swamping her senses. But at last she managed to drag herself free.

"How dare you?" she cried furiously,

and turned and fled in a panic to get away from him, stumbling across the patio on unsteady legs, through the lounge and out to the staircase.

In the sanctuary of her bedroom, Lynn stood with her back against the door, her breast heaving, her whole body hot with shame. She heaped curses upon her own weakness, and upon the man who had so cynically taken advantage of it.

Damn him, she raged. Damn Brett Sackville for demonstrating with such consummate ease that she, Lynn Forster, could be conquered as readily as any other woman of his acquaintance. Thank heaven she had realised in time the danger she was in, and that it was *she*, not *he*, who had brought the seduction scene to an end. She was appalled to realise the intensity of her emotions, which had swept her along on a tidal wave of longing for this man — a man who felt nothing more for her than the contempt he felt for *all* women.

A shudder ran through her as she wondered what would have happened had not that stab of cold reality mercifully saved her in time. Would he have openly mocked her, pouring scorn on all those highflown principles of hers which he had so easily and uncaringly pushed aside? At least she had been spared that humiliation! But it was a small sop to her peace of mind, when her pounding heart and trembling body left her in little doubt of how close Brett had come to total victory. And Lynn was painfully conscious that he was just as aware of this as she was.

★ ★ ★

In those first sleepless hours of the night, Lynn made up her mind a dozen times that she could stay no longer at *La Casa Española*. Tomorrow morning she would pack her suitcase and leave, giving Brett Sackville the name of a reliable picture restorer who would finish the job she had only just begun.

And a dozen times she changed her mind. To leave would be to hand him an easy victory. He would know — and delight in the knowledge — that she was leaving because she could not trust herself to resist him. Besides which, warned a practical inner voice, the comparatively small world of art restoration wouldn't fail to note that Lynn Forster had abandoned the first big commission she'd undertaken since her father's death.

To stay here and see this through was a challenge, she decided, a challenge to herself as a professional, and a challenge to herself as a woman. She would demonstrate to Brett Sackville, by an attitude of cool, calm detachment, that a momentary weakness on her part proved nothing, and that her principles and beliefs stood firm.

Later, when it was long past midnight, Lynn heard the soft tread of his footsteps on the landing outside her room. She chided herself for having left her bedside light on. No doubt it showed under her door, and he would regard that as gratifying proof that she was lying restless and awake.

She heard a quiet click as he closed his bedroom door, then the faint sounds as he moved around the room. After a few minutes everything was quiet and she guessed he must be in bed. Switching off her light, Lynn lay there staring into the darkness, conscious of Brett Sackville's extreme proximity. Having been inside his room, she knew that but for the wall between them, she could have reached out her hand and touched his head where it lay upon his pillow, again twining her fingers into his springy, dark hair.

Lynn remained awake for hours. The first pale light of dawn was touching the edges of the magenta curtains when at last she fell into a troubled slumber. In her dreams she heard again the lyrical outpouring of the Rachmaninov concerto and felt herself being transported once more to the unknown, unfathomable realm of sensual desire.

A quick glance at her wristwatch when she finally wakened told her it was almost nine-thirty! Appalled, Lynn jumped out of bed and hastily washed and dressed, pulling on her working jeans and a clean white shirt. The face that stared back at her from the dressing-table mirror showed the ravages of a sleepless, dream-tormented night. Make-up helped to conceal this a little, but as she hurried downstairs Lynn was uncomfortably aware that she looked far from her best.

Hearing her, Mrs. Mackenzie popped her head round the kitchen door. She smiled at Lynn, and said, "That was a fine wee lie-in you had! I didn't disturb you, because it's Saturday and I knew you must need the rest, considering how hard you've been working all this week."

"I'm sorry if I've interfered with your timetable, Mrs. Mackenzie," Lynn apologised, adding falsely, "I just slept like a log all night."

"Never you mind about that, lassie. Mr. Brett is late for his breakfast, too . . . he's just having a swim. He'll not be long, so you won't mind waiting a wee while, will you?"

"No . . . no, of course not," Lynn stammered, feeling dismayed. She'd thought that by coming down so late she would at least have escaped the intimacy of sharing the breakfast table with him. But no such luck! Resigning herself to the inevitable, she picked up a morning paper and sat with it on the patio.

After ten minutes Brett Sackville appeared on the flagged path leading from the pool. He wore crisp fawn slacks and a pale-blue short-sleeved shirt, with leather sandals on his bare feet. The fine dark hairs on his muscular forearms glinted in the sunshine.

"Hallo!" he greeted her in a cheerful voice. "So you're up, then! You should have joined me in the pool."

Lynn shuddered inwardly . . . that was something she had no intention of ever doing again, no matter how persuasive he was. Giving him a faint, uncertain smile, she said,

"I really should have been at work ages ago. I'm afraid I overslept disgracefully this morning."

"Why was that? Did you have a bad night?" His eyes were shrewd, searching.

She folded the newspaper and stood up. "I suppose that I was just overtired," she said evasively.

"Perhaps!" He hesitated a moment, then began, "Look, about last night . . . "

"Mr. Sackville, I would prefer to forget last night," she interposed with quiet dignity, and preceded him into the dining-room. Hearing them, Mrs. Mackenzie followed with a large pot of coffee, its delicious aroma filling the room.

Brett Sackville waited until the housekeeper had withdrawn. "Why, Miss Forster?"

"Why what?"

"Why do you want to forget last night?"

His directness disconcerted her. "I . . . I would have thought that was obvious," she replied, somehow keeping her voice level.

"Not to me it isn't!"

"If you think that what happened in some way discredits the views I expressed, you are quite mistaken," she remarked, digging her spoon into the grapefruit before her. "A momentary lapse is irrelevant."

"Is that all it was — a momentary lapse?" One dark eyebrow lifted in irony.

"What else, for heaven's sake?" She paused briefly, then plunged on, "If you read some deeper meaning into the incident, then perhaps you can explain why I so quickly brought it to an end."

"Oh, very easily! It's part of every woman's instinctive equipment to know that nothing challenges a man more effectively than a seeming advance and a sudden coy retreat. The ruse works everytime without fail! You now intrigue me far more than if you hadn't fled to your room with every appearance of outraged innocence."

The colour rushed to Lynn's cheeks, but she refused to rise to his bait.

"You are talking nonsense!" she said curtly.

"Permit me to be the judge of my own reactions, Miss Forster."

"As long as you leave me to judge mine!" she hit back.

"By all means! I only ask you to be honest with yourself . . . if that's possible for *any* woman."

They were both so engrossed in their battle of words that they didn't hear the car which drew up in front of the house. Their first intimation of a visitor was when the dining-room door burst open and a slender, raven-haired woman walked in, curtly dismissing Mrs. Mackenzie, who had come to announce her, with an imperious flick of the hand.

"Juanita! What a surprise!" Brett Sackville had quickly risen to his feet, pushing back his chair.

"Oh yes, I am in no doubt of that, Brett!" Black eyes flashed at him jealously. "Who is this . . . this person with whom I find you breakfasting in the middle of the morning?"

He glanced at Lynn, almost as if he'd forgotten her presence. "This is Miss Forster, Juanita. She is staying here while she restores those horse paintings in my study." For Lynn's benefit, he added, "This is Señora Vazquez, a friend of mine from Spain."

Lynn had already noticed that the newcomer wore a heavy gold band on the third finger of her left hand. In reply to the introduction she murmured a polite, smiling greeting, but the Spanish woman was regarding her with the deepest suspicion. It was clear that she had at once noted the telltale signs in Lynn's appearance which pointed to a night with little sleep.

"'Restores' . . . what is this, Brett?"

she enquired sulkily.

"The condition of the paintings has deteriorated over the years," he explained. "Miss Forster is an expert at putting such things right."

The black eyes were slitted now, long lashes sweeping down like shutters as she sized up the situation. "You employ her, Brett, yes . . . she works for you? Then why is she not at work now, might I ask, instead of enjoying a cosy *tête-a-tête* with you over the breakfast table?"

Determined not to let anything connected with Brett Sackville ruffle her, Lynn stood up and made to leave the room, murmuring something to the effect that she had been on the point of going anyway. But he abruptly motioned her back into her chair.

"You've had no toast, Miss Forster, and your first cup of coffee is only half-finished. Won't you join us, Juanita?" Without waiting for an answer he called Mrs. Mackenzie to bring another cup and saucer, then continued to his guest,

"Now explain to me how it is that you've arrived here so unexpectedly. I had no idea you were even coming to England."

"Perhaps you wish me not to come?" she pouted.

"Don't be foolish, you know I'm always delighted to see you, Juanita. But how did you know I was in Sussex?"

Sitting down, Señora Vazquez slid her chair nearer to his.

"I arrived just this morning, on an early flight. I telephoned your flat from the airport, but the porter told me you had been staying here all this past week. So I took a taxi at once!"

"What an impulsive girl you are!" he laughed.

Her voice was silk-soft, deep in her throat. "You make me impulsive, *caro*. We have been parted for so long!"

"Come now, it must be less than two months since I last saw you," he chided. "And I shall be in Spain again next week."

Lynn, who had been determinedly chewing buttered toast, trying to look disinterested in their conversation, was jolted by his words. He had said nothing about leaving England. So from sometime next week she would have *La Casa Española* to herself — apart from the Mackenzies. Why, she wondered, didn't the prospect fill her with a sense of relief?

Juanita had moved still nearer to Brett and, ignoring the presence of a third party, she was unashamedly resting her head against his shoulder and allowing her long, olive-brown fingers to toy with the gold medallion that hung around his neck. It sickened Lynn to see a member of her sex throwing herself at a man so blatantly. Brett glanced momentarily in her direction, and Lynn imagined a glint of triumph in his dark eyes. Very deliberately, she reached across the table for the silver coffee pot and refilled her cup, trying to keep her hand from shaking as she did so.

"Next week, Brett!" Juanita's tone was reproachful. "But I could not wait until next week, *caro mío*! So I come now, and when you leave for *España*, I shall return with you, no?"

Lynn could stand it no longer. Leaving her coffee cup full she jumped to her feet so hastily that she slopped some into the saucer, and banged her thigh painfully against the table leg. Muttering an excuse about it being high time she started work, she almost ran from the room.

But when she reached her improvised studio, Lynn stood for a long time at the easel staring into space. A woman like Juanita Vazquez seemed tailor-made for Brett Sackville, and he for her. Both of them were hard, selfish people, manipulating life for their own ends. She supposed that Juanita was a widow and that she'd chosen Brett as a second husband who could provide her with sufficient wealth and status in the world to satisfy her greed. And as for Brett . . . he was probably only too well aware of this fact, using Juanita for his own amusement while all the time determined to remain free and unfettered or, as he had put it, unscathed! Well, it was nothing whatever to do with her, Lynn thought savagely, shaking a bottle of the varnish solvent so fiercely that the stopper came loose and a few drops of the liquid spilled on the floor.

An hour later, the door opened without any preliminary knock and Juanita walked into the room, for all the world as if she were mistress of the house. She had changed, Lynn noticed, from the smartly-tailored blue suit she'd been wearing on her arrival, into figure-hugging, cream linen pants and an orange mini top which left her slim midriff bare. Coming forward, she perched herself against the edge of the table and regarded Lynn with haughty condescension.

"Do you ride, Señorita Forster?"

Lynn broke off work, surprised at the question. "You mean . . . horses?"

"But of course!"

"Well, not really!" She was about to explain that she'd had little opportunity for riding since her childhood. But the other girl cut across her.

"I ride as though I had been born in the saddle . . . as I almost was! My father, you see, owns one of the largest studs in Andalusia — he breeds fine Arabs. I find it difficult to imagine not being a horsewoman." She gestured scornfully towards the painting on the easel before Lynn. "This thing you are so 'expert' at . . . it seems not very feminine to me."

"Really?" Lynn managed to inject indifference into her voice. She picked up a new cotton wool swab, dipped it in the jar of solvent, and commenced the gentle rolling movement that safely removed the old and discoloured film of varnish without damage to the paint layer underneath. "I see no reason why a woman should not do this work as well as a man. Anything that requires years of practice to master must surely have its own satisfaction, whichever your sex."

"Years of practice!" Juanita echoed scathingly. "Really, Señorita Forster ... you may make fools of men with your pretty face and simpering ways! But *I* can understand you only too well. This work you do is no more skilled than ... than the cleaning of a window!"

Before Lynn realised her intention, Juanita had grabbed up a ball of cotton wool, dipped it into the solvent, and commenced scrubbing furiously at the surface of the painting.

"There, you see!" she exclaimed triumphantly, as the sage-green of a lady's riding habit gleamed with fresh brilliance. "The dirt comes off easily. Already I have cleaned in five seconds more than you would do in one hour."

Appalled, Lynn snatched the cotton wool from the other girl and tossed it aside. Hastily, she applied some of the special restraining agent she always kept handy in order to prevent the solvent that Juanita had applied so liberally and so forcefully from softening more of the delicate paint and further damaging the picture.

"How dare you come in here and interfere," she cried angrily. "You could easily ruin the painting doing that, and I would be held responsible."

In face of Lynn's unexpected wrath, Juanita had paled. But she quickly rallied.

"Oh, do not pretend with me! See, that part I rubbed is cleaner than anything you have done."

"Only because you took half the paint off with it," Lynn exploded. She bent and picked up the discarded cotton wool from where it had fallen on the floor. "If you don't believe me, look at this . . . where else do you think that green has come from? Of all the idiots I've ever come across, you take the prize!"

Neither girl had heard Brett Sackville enter the room. They both started at the sound of his amused chuckle.

"I think Juanita is a little jealous of finding you established at *La Casa Española*, Miss Forster," he remarked ironically. "Shall we tell her she has no cause for jealousy? You are completely dedicated to your profession, are you not . . . until, that is, the man of your girlish dreams sweeps into your life, and you abandon everything for love! I wonder who the lucky man will be?"

Sorely tried, Lynn drew herself up to her full height.

"Whatever you choose to think, either of you, this work happens to demand a great deal of concentration. I should be grateful if I might be allowed to get on with it in peace."

He inclined his head. "Fair enough! Actually, I only came to say that Juanita and I have decided to go riding this afternoon. I was just about to phone the stables for two mounts when it occurred to me that you might care to join us."

"She does not ride!" Juanita cut in,

with spiteful satisfaction. "She has told me this just now."

"Is that so, Miss Forster?"

Lynn hesitated. She was tempted to score off Juanita by saying that as a child she had ridden a good deal, and been praised for her excellent seat. But this would look like currying favour with him, the very idea of which she scorned. Besides, seeing him and the Spanish woman together sickened her, and the less time she spent in their company the better.

"No, I don't ride," she said evenly.

"A pity!" The dark eyes were full of mockery as he went on, "It's a fine way of taking exercise . . . almost as good as swimming. Now you cannot tell me that you don't swim, Miss Forster. I have the evidence of my own eyes that you do. And moreover, you came here equipped for it, did you not? Most effectively equipped, I might add!"

Juanita was looking from the one to the other of them, not understanding what Brett was alluding to. But Lynn understood only too well! That too-revealing yellow bikini ... he was suggesting that she wore it provocatively, as a snare to entice a man into her trap.

As he and the Spanish girl turned to go, Lynn determined that as soon as they were out of the way she was going straight upstairs to her room. She would take that wretched swimsuit and tear it into tiny pieces. Never again would he have an opportunity of sneering at her motives while his eyes stripped her body until she felt naked before him.

# 3

LYNN slept remarkably well, and awoke to a Sunday morning full of bright sunshine and a medley of birdsong. She glanced at her wristwatch and saw that it was still not quite seven-thirty. If she got up now, she decided, she could be out of the house before Brett Sackville and Juanita were about. It would be unthinkable to have breakfast with them and be forced to listen to them discussing their Saturday evening out at some nightspot along the coast.

She had managed to keep out of their way fairly well yesterday after that unpleasant encounter in the garden room. The two of them had been out for lunch, and the only other time Lynn saw them that day was when she was enjoying a quiet cup of tea which Mrs. Mackenzie had insisted on serving on the patio.

"You work much too much," the housekeeper had told Lynn reprovingly. "Everyone needs a break every now and then. Shall I bring you some of my gingerbread — it's just hot out of the oven?"

Lynn smiled, patting her tummy ruefully. "How can I resist? But I'll put on pounds and pounds if I stay here long."

"A wee bit of building up would do you no harm, lassie! Not that you're thin, mind," she added quickly. "Just about right, I'd say, and not only in your figure. You've got a nice nature . . . unlike some I could name!"

Lynn's feeling of contentment had been abruptly shattered when the others arrived on the scene, still in their riding clothes. Juanita looked stunning in fine worsted jodhpurs and a cream silk blouse. Brett Sackville, still warm from the exercise, had unbuttoned his shirt almost to the waist, and Lynn could glimpse the hard lean body underneath, the dark curling hairs on his chest damp with perspiration.

"Tea! That's a good idea!" he exclaimed, and called to Mrs. Mackenzie to make another pot.

They both sat down and Lynn, determined to keep her poise, asked coolly and politely if they had enjoyed their ride.

"Very much!" he said, leaning back in his chair and regarding her with a lazy smile. "It's a pity you didn't come, too."

"She could never have kept up with us," Juanita observed pointedly. "We ride hard, Señor Sackville and I, Señorita Forster; we live life to the full! If you ever take up riding you should choose a docile mount that needs no mastery."

Lynn seethed inwardly, knowing that the remark was doubly meant as a veiled warning that a man like Brett Sackville was not for the likes of her. Well, she would find an opportunity to inform the Spanish girl that she didn't want him, not at any price.

Changing the subject abruptly, Lynn said, "Mr. Sackville, I rather wanted a word with you about the paintings. On closer examination I find that one of them is showing slight signs of cleavage . . . "

"Cleavage!" He pounced with relish. "I've always thought that the word 'cleavage' was used to describe a particularly delectable portion of the female anatomy." His gaze lingered knowledgeably just below the neckline of Lynn's T-shirt, causing her to flush.

"I used the term in its technical sense," she pointed out, grimly clinging to her fraying calm. "It refers to a condition where a layer of paint becomes separated from its canvas support. It would be advisable to have this dealt with, or it will grow worse over the years."

"Is it something you could see to?" he enquired.

"Oh yes! But on that particular picture there's rather more work involved than I originally estimated. You see, cleavage isn't always apparent until you actually begin on restoration work," she added defensively. "Shall I jot down what is required, and the probable cost, so you can consider whether it's worth having it done?"

"As you wish." he said, as if he could hardly care less what she did about it.

After this exchange, Lynn had returned to work in her studio, and she hadn't seen either of them since. Eating her dinner alone in the dining-room, she'd suddenly found the deep hush of the countryside depressing. She could hear the faint murmur of the Mackenzies' voices from the kitchen regions, and somehow that seemed to accentuate her loneliness.

Afterwards, in the lounge, she had switched on the television set, but realised after ten minutes or so that she hadn't been taking in a bit of what had been happening on the screen. Switching it off again, she began to wander around the room. Perhaps some music would soothe her, she thought restlessly. She went to the record player and found to her vexation that Brett had left the Rachmaninov disc on the turntable. She certainly wouldn't play *that*; she doubted if she would ever want to hear it again. The memory of those fateful minutes on the patio, with the sweet fragrance of a summer evening all around her and a silver moon riding silently above the Downs, went searing through Lynn. The poignant theme of the concerto, so well-remembered and once so precious to her, pulsed in her brain insistently. She could feel again the terrifying sweetness of his kisses and the virile strength of his hard, masculine body against hers, destroying her will to resist him . . . With an exclamation of dismay, she had turned and run from the room, fleeing from the torturing memory just as, the previous night, she had fled from the reality.

This morning, Lynn had managed

to get things in better perspective. Never again would the moonlight and a simple little piece of music — as she denigratingly described the magnificent classic concerto in her thoughts — be allowed to undermine her common sense.

She sought out Mrs. Mackenzie, already busy in her kitchen, and together they packed a picnic basket for Lynn to take with her. Then, after a hasty breakfast of coffee and toast and marmalade, Lynn eased the dear old Rover from the garage and set off through the leafy Sussex lanes, dappled with patterns of sunlight and shadow. She was heading for the coast, feeling a sudden need to be among people — ordinary, happy people enjoying a summer Sunday by the sea.

And yet, on the beach, an even more intense loneliness descended upon her. The obvious gaiety and happiness of those around her only underlined her own sense of isolation. Perhaps she should have gone back to London today, and invited friends round to the flat for a meal. But it was too late now; and anyway, the thought didn't really appeal. In the end, giving up all attempt to lose herself in the paperback she'd bought, she strolled among the sand dunes and found a quiet spot to eat her picnic lunch. Afterwards, she headed for the Downs and, parking the car, walked a little on the centuries-old track that led for miles all along the ridge of hills. She paused constantly, sometimes to admire a view of the sparkling channel or, facing inland, to gain a panorama of the gentle Sussex weald, green and wooded, basking peacefully in the warm sunshine. She spent several minutes searching with her eyes for *La Casa Española*, but perhaps it was concealed by trees. She tried to picture the house as it was at this moment. Brett Sackville and Juanita would be at the pool, no doubt. The Spanish girl would look devastating in a swimsuit created by one of the continental masters of *haute couture*;

and the man, clad briefly in trunks, his long lean body stretched out lazily in a lounge chair, would be regarding her with a gleam of appreciation in his dark eyes.

Or would they, instead, be clasped in one another's arms?

The air on the hilltop seemed suddenly to turn chill, despite the blazing sun. Turning, Lynn wended her way back to where she had left the car. Although it was still early, she unconsciously took the most direct route back to The Spanish House.

Mrs. Mackenzie heard her drive in, and came to greet her in the hall.

"You're back then, lassie! I wasn't sure if you'd be wanting dinner this evening, or if you'd be staying out."

"No, I'll be in."

"Aye, well now . . . what would you fancy? There's kidneys I could sauté, with bacon and mushrooms. Or how about a lovely cut of cold beef with salad?"

"Oh, I'll be happy to have whatever

Mr. Sackville and Señora Vazquez are having," Lynn said.

The housekeeper's face registered surprise, which quickly cleared. "Of course, you don't know! They're not here, lassie . . . they went off directly after lunch."

"They've gone out for the whole day, you mean?" queried Lynn, not knowing whether to be pleased or sorry.

"No, they're off to Spain! Leastways," she amended, "they're going to London first, and flying out tomorrow or the next day."

Lynn couldn't take it in properly. She'd known they were going to Spain sometime this coming week, but she hadn't been prepared to find them already gone.

"How . . . how long will Mr. Sackville be away for?" she enquired weakly.

Mrs. Mackenzie shrugged. "A few days, maybe . . . or more likely several weeks. It varies a lot, depending on what he finds needing to be done out there." She gave Lynn a knowing look. "And how much he's enjoying himself, I expect!"

Lynn faltered, "That . . . that means I shall possibly have finished the work here before he returns."

"Oh yes, about that, lassie . . . Mr. Brett told me to tell you to send your bill to his secretary, and she'll settle it."

It all seemed so casual, so uncaring — even brutally indifferent.

"I . . . I was going to talk with him about some extra work that's needed on one of the paintings," she said chokily.

"That's right! He said not to worry . . . just go ahead and do whatever you think is needed."

Bewildered, Lynn wandered upstairs to her room and stood for ages at the window, staring out. She had the complete run of the house now, she could wander at will without risk of encountering the derisive gaze of those disturbing dark eyes. She could become engrossed in her fascinating work each day, free of the knowledge that the evening would bring him back from London to torment and humiliate her over dinner, reminding her constantly that she had almost lost herself in the heady intoxication of his kiss.

But, strangely, she felt no satisfaction at the prospect, no pleasure in contemplating her new freedom. The thought of the time ahead already weighed heavily on her, the few weeks she would be obliged to remain here seeming to stretch like an infinity.

Because Brett Sackville would not be here? It was shameful, she told herself angrily, to be so deeply in the grip of a purely physical attraction . . . a longing to be in the arms of a man for whom she should have felt nothing but contempt. That would negate every principle she stood for and lend support to his own base philosophy that pure, unselfish love was a myth.

Yet it was impossible to deny that

her whole being cried out for the feel of his arms about her, his warm body throbbing against hers. It was futile to pretend that her own lips were not burning for the sensual promise of his lips, sending delight shivering through her. Maybe, Lynn thought bitterly, this was his final victory over her . . . to go away and leave her now, aware of the intense yearning he had aroused within her. What vast amusement he must be enjoying at this moment . . . better even, perhaps, than if she had actually succumbed to him that night instead of belatedly jerking to her senses in those final moments. Yet another woman conquered would mean no more to Brett Sackville than a brief and soon-forgotten pleasure, but a woman destroyed in her own eyes — as he must know *she* was destroyed — would surely give him an exciting new experience to boost his arrogant male ego.

★ ★ ★

The sun blazed down again all day Monday, but instead of feeling pleasantly warm, Lynn's sun-room studio struck her as unbearably hot and stuffy. Although wearing just a T-shirt and thin cotton jeans, with all the windows and doors thrown open, she found it almost impossible to concentrate on her work.

Even when the sun had set, there still didn't seem to be enough air to breathe. Lynn arranged with Mrs. Mackenzie for a very light meal to be served on the patio . . . just some cold chicken and a green salad, with a lemon sherbet to follow. Afterwards she sat over her coffee, flicking through the pages of a 'Country Life' magazine, but even that called for too much effort. She felt strangely restless. Or rather, she corrected herself, exhausted. And no wonder, of course, for doing such finicky work in this kind of heat was very demanding.

An early night was the best treatment, she decided, and she went straight upstairs to her bedroom. Although she had bathed before dinner she took a shower now, allowing the cool water to course luxuriously down her skin for several minutes before reluctantly stepping out and towelling herself dry. In her coolest, wispiest nightdress she lingered at the wide open window. The moon, a huge circle floating in the velvety night sky, was brushing the gardens with its silvery light.

On a sudden impulse she drew on her sprigged-cotton robe and slid her feet into sandals. Opening the door, she listened for a moment. Very faintly, she could hear canned laughter coming from the Mackenzies' quarters . . . a TV comedy show by the sound of it. So she would have the gardens entirely to herself, to wander in and enjoy the sensation of the cool night air on her face. Perhaps it would help rid her of this strange feeling of restiveness and allow her to get some sleep tonight.

Outside, it was very calm and still. In contrast to the bright moonlight, the shadows cast by trees and shrubs were densely dark and mysterious. As she crossed the lawns the air was filled with the fragrance of night-scented flowers . . . azaleas and jasmine and, sweetest and most evocative of all, the honeysuckle that had twined its tendrils into a trellis arch.

At the boundary hedge, Lynn paused by the stile which led to the grove of young oak saplings. Resting her hands on the top rail, she listened to the whisper of the little stream which skirted this side of *La Casa Española*'s gardens, and from somewhere a little way off came the sweet trilling of a nightingale. Apart from this, the only sound to be heard was the occasional swish of a car going by in the lane on the far side of the house.

The minutes drifted by and, as Lynn drank in the beauty of the summer night, she felt curiously detached from herself. As if her unhappiness was being held at bay . . .

On the springy turf she heard no

sound of a footfall. The voice coming from just behind her crashed into her brain with sudden violence.

"You look as if you're waiting for someone, but I can't imagine who."

Lynn froze, in shock and disbelief. It sounded so real, yet surely it could only be her imagination playing cruel tricks? She spun round quickly, so quickly that the thin cotton of her robe caught on the stile's rough timber and she heard the sound of it ripping.

"What . . . what are you doing here?" she stammered at Brett. He stood scarcely three feet away from her, the shirt he was wearing gleaming whitely in the moonlight, while his eyes were two dark pools of shadow from which she caught the glint of irony.

"Looking for you!" he said. "Though I hadn't expected to find you so seductively attired, not at this time of the evening."

"I . . . I was tired and I decided to go to bed early," she explained.

"Indeed?" He took a step nearer,

and she pressed herself back against the wooden rail. "So why did you not retire to bed?"

I thought I'd come outside for a breath of air first," she said, miserably aware of how feeble an excuse that must sound. "It . . . it seemed so dreadfully hot and stuffy indoors."

"Ah yes," he agreed sardonically. "These summer nights of almost tropical heat do make one restless, don't they? In fact," he added with a soft chuckle, "they can play the very devil with one's imagination. However, there's no need for you to rely on your imagination any longer, for I am here in the flesh."

"Whatever gives you the idea that I was thinking about you?" she retorted, with an attempt at coolness, though her heart was hammering against her ribs.

"Weren't you?"

"Certainly not. I've got far more important things to give my mind to, Mr. Sackville."

"Such as what?"

"For one thing, my job happens to

demand a great deal of concentrated thought and planning . . . "

"Which you find best accomplished by wandering through my garden at night, dressed only in a few sexy wisps of fabric which are cunningly designed to conceal just enough of your delectable body to set a man's passions alight."

"Don't be absurd," Lynn said, trying desperately to keep her voice steady. "How could I have intended any such thing, considering there was no man here . . . except for Mr. Mackenzie."

"But there is now," Brett pointed out remorselessly, "And I can assure you, Lynn Forster, that the effect you're having on me is exactly as I have described."

Aware that she would be unable to escape without pushing past him — which she doubted he would permit in his present mood — Lynn spoke desperately, "You didn't answer my question, Mr. Sackville. What brings you down here . . . to Sussex, I mean?"

"Do I have to account for my presence?" he asked sarcastically. "*La Casa Española* happens to be my house, you know."

"But Mrs. Mackenzie said that you'd gone to Spain. Or at least she said to London first, but I got the definite impression that you weren't intending to come back here before going to Spain."

"I'm not obliged to keep my housekeeper informed of every move I make," he said witheringly. "As it happens, I changed my mind and decided to return here this evening . . . because you and I have some unfinished business to attend to."

"Unfinished business?" she echoed, with a sinking heart. "But I thought you'd left instructions that I was to go ahead and do whatever I thought necessary to restore the paintings properly."

"I wasn't referring to the paintings."

"What, then?" asked Lynn weakly.

He gave a low laugh. "You going off

for the day like that yesterday achieved just the effect you planned, my dear Lynn. My interest was vastly aroused, and I had to come and see you this evening to pick up where we left off the other night."

"Where . . . where we left off?" she faltered nervously.

"Don't you remember . . . you gave me a demonstration of how you react to a man's kiss when you feel nothing whatever for him. I found it quite fascinating, and I've come back for a repeat performance of your indifference."

Lynn's throat was suddenly dry, and she had to swallow before she could speak. "I'm not stopping here to bandy words with you. Let me pass, please."

"Not until we've shared that kiss," he countered relentlessly. Then in a gentler voice, he went on, "That's all I'm asking of you, Lynn . . . for the moment. An open acknowledgement that you want to be kissed by me every bit as much as I want to kiss you."

"But that's not true!"

"Do I have to prove it all over again?" he said, in a tone of weary impatience. "Perhaps you're one of those women who enjoy their lovemaking better when they're overpowered. But take care, my dear Lynn . . . if you rouse me too far you might get more than you bargained for."

He reached out as he was speaking, and Lynn felt his fingers close on her shoulders in a grip that brooked no denial. In wild panic, she stammered, "There . . . there's somebody watching us . . . "

"Where?" he said, half turning and relaxing his hold. Lynn took advantage of her momentary freedom by scrambling over the stile. She heard a smothered exclamation from Brett as she ran across the little rustic bridge that spanned the stream and plunged recklessly into the grove of young oak trees. But already she was realising her foolish mistake. There could be no escape this way, not for someone dressed as scantily as she was. She tried to hold the billowing material of her robe more closely about her, but brambles snagged it as she fled along the path.

Brett was coming after her and, in desperation, Lynn increased her pace. Then suddenly she was caught in the snare of a bramble that was trailing right across the pathway. She tried to drag her robe away, but it was caught by the thorns in at least half a dozen places.

"Please," she begged, "just help me get free."

"Willingly." She felt his hands running over her body as he explored the situation. Then he announced firmly, "There's only one thing for it, you'll have to slip out of that robe. That way, I'll be able to disentangle it easily."

"No!" she objected. "I'm not going to."

"If you don't, it will take a great deal longer," he warned. "And anything might happen in the process."

"Oh, very well," Lynn said miserably. "But afterwards, I'm going straight back indoors. Is that clearly understood?"

Brett didn't reply as he turned his attention to her robe. He made no effort to hurry but took his time, constantly glancing up at her with some cheerful comment that it was coming along nicely. As she waited with growing impatience, Lynn realised to her chagrin how horribly exposed she was, standing there in a shaft of moonlight in nothing but her sheer, knee-length nightdress. Quickly, she stepped back into the shadow of a tree.

"There," Brett announced at last. "It's free now, and I've managed to avoid doing any extra damage."

"Thank you," Lynn gritted through clenched teeth. But as she reached out to take the robe from him, she found that her wrist was caught in a vise-like grip.

"Let me go!" she cried. "What do you think you're doing?"

His arms closed about her, steel strong, locking her against him so that her breasts were crushed against the wall of his chest.

"I'm claiming my reward," he murmured into her hair. "Surely you agree that I at least deserve the kiss I came here for, after being so helpful?"

"But . . . but it was your fault that my robe got caught in the brambles," she protested, outraged.

"Correction!" he drawled. "It was entirely your own fault, for pretending to take flight from a wicked seducer. It was patently obvious to us both that you'd never get away from me by rushing off through this wood. It was an open invitation for me to follow and catch you."

"It was nothing of the kind," Lynn said furiously. But every second he held her there, clamped against him, she became more distressingly aware that her own treacherous instincts were leaping within her. There was a sensual excitement about the pressure of his hard, lean body that threatened to overwhelm her senses. In a desperate attempt to break the potent enchantment, she threw out, "What would Juanita think, I wonder, if she knew that you were behaving like this?"

"Juanita is in London," he said dismissively, "and you are here, my lovely Lynn."

His fingers roamed slowly up and down her back, leaving a tingling trail of fire across her skin wherever he touched her. The flimsy nightdress was no obstacle; she might have been completely naked for all the barrier it made between them.

"Suppose . . . " she sobbed, "suppose I were to shout for the Mackenzies? How would you like them to catch you here with me?"

A laugh bubbled deep in his throat. "I think you would be the one to be embarrassed, Lynn. But if you don't believe me — go ahead and try. Shout as much as you like."

"Why are you so hateful?" she said despairingly.

"Poor Lynn!" he mocked. "Let's see how hateful you really find me."

Without warning, he bent his head and pressed his lips to hers. She struggled weakly, to no avail, for Brett only kissed her the harder, forcing her lips apart to seek the inner sweetness of her mouth. Dismayingly, Lynn felt the feeble shreds of her resistance slipping from her grasp. The arms that should have been pushing him away came up and wound around his neck, drawing him even closer. She felt the surging heat of his passion, and her own body responded with a desperate yearning which threw all discretion to the winds. No longer needing to hold her in restraint, Brett's hand slid up to cup her breast, his fingertips finding the nipple and caressing it to a taut, tense peak, sending a shiver of wild delight through her veins. As he drew his lips away, her head fell back and she let out a low moan of ecstasy.

Brett said softly, triumphantly, "So! Do you still maintain that you find me hateful, Lynn?"

It was the arrogance in his voice that saved her. The feelings of shame which had ebbed away now came rushing back in a flood. With a violent push, she thrust herself out of his arms.

"You . . . you're despicable," she sobbed. "Just because you're strong, and . . . and you can subdue a woman physically, you think it gives you the right to . . . to do as you please with her."

"If you honestly believe that," Brett responded evenly, "then you're taking a mighty big risk, throwing abuse at me when I've got you at my mercy. But you've given yourself away, my dear Lynn. It's clear to me now that if I were to make a really determined effort, you could no more hold out against me than you could stop yourself from breathing. These momentary lapses of yours, as you choose to call them, are very revealing. They show me what a warm, exciting woman lies behind the façade of cool efficiency you endeavour to present to the world."

He had let her robe fall to the ground, and Lynn stooped for it quickly and drew it on. Feeling that much less vulnerable with this extra covering, she was emboldened to say, "I suppose it makes you feel really great, to have proved that I possess a human weakness . . . "

"I wouldn't call it a weakness, Lynn. The possession of a deeply sensual nature is a strength, a strength a woman should glory in."

"No doubt," she said cuttingly, "you speak from your wide experience of women."

"As I said, I've had enough experience to know that basically all women are the same deep down," he replied. "They think it's their role in life to play every man they meet as an angler plays a fish, pitting their wits against his to land him on the shore, their helpless victim. And they don't like it when they come up against a man who can beat them at their own game."

"What a very low opinion you have of my sex!" Her heart was thudding painfully, but somehow she found enough control to say, in a firm, decisive voice, "Perhaps I'd better put you right, Mr. Brett Sackville, as far as I'm concerned. To me you are no more than a philanderer, a cheap seducer, and I've got your measure now. If it were not for the fact that you'll be off again tomorrow, and presumably won't be back from Spain until I've finished my work on the paintings, I wouldn't stay here and do the job."

"Because you'd be afraid of succumbing to my fatal attractions?" he suggested.

"No!" she hit back. "Because I wouldn't care to spend several weeks in the company of a man I utterly despise. As it is . . . "

"You've got it wrong about me leaving here tomorrow," Brett interrupted. "I'm returning to London tonight."

A sudden feeling of chill gripped

her. She tried to shake it off by saying sarcastically, "Hurrying back to Juanita, I suppose, having failed with me? Doubtless you'll find her more amenable. But I advise you to take great care if you're so anxious not to be caught by Señora Vazquez. From what I saw of her, I'd say that she's a very determined lady."

"And of course her hook is so enticingly baited, is it not?" he drawled. "But you needn't worry on my account, Lynn. I'm in no danger of being caught by Juanita — or by anyone else."

Lynn bit back the stinging retort that rose to her lips, unhappily aware that this man was invariably able to cap whatever she said. When Brett reached out suddenly and caught her shoulders again, she conquered the impulse to struggle and let herself go utterly limp.

"So you're not going to fight me this time?" he asked in surprise.

"What would be the point? I can't force you to let go of me."

For a few moments he held her, staring intently into her eyes. Then, abruptly, he let her go.

"You won't succeed in your scheming, you know," he said in a harsh, cruel voice. "I freely admit that I came back here tonight because you had intrigued me, as you intended to. But that's all over now. I find your stupid feminine game exceedingly boring, Miss Forster. You can stay and finish the job you're here to do, or walk out on an unfinished contract — whichever you please. I don't give a damn because, in either case, you'll be long gone before I return to England."

With that he turned and strode off along the path, leaving Lynn in a state of numbed shock. A small cloud had drifted across the moon, cutting off its clear brilliance, and almost at once his tall figure was swallowed up in the darkness of the trees.

Shivering miserably, Lynn stood there unmoving for long minutes before slowly making her fumbling way back to the house. She supposed that Brett must have stopped to have a word with the Mackenzies, but before she was halfway across the lawn she heard the sound of his car bursting into life. Then she heard the gravel crunching beneath its wheels as he accelerated violently and roared away into the night.

# 4

LYNN immersed herself in work, spending long hours each day at her easel. Mrs. Mackenzie tut-tutted at such extreme dedication, warning Lynn that she would make herself ill if she weren't careful. But Lynn knew that only by concentrating hard on her demanding task until she was tired out and ready to flop into bed could she hope to hold at bay those treacherous thoughts of Brett Sackville.

Even so, they came creeping in the instant her guard was lowered. The picture on the easel before her would dissolve into mist and a mental picture would take its place, a picture of a tall, handsome man with a lean, hard body and craggy face, from which dark eyes stared out at her mockingly. With an angry gesture Lynn would shrug off the disturbing image and apply herself once more to her task.

The following Friday afternoon, she was vaguely aware of the sound of a car drawing up outside. Thinking it must be just a tradesman she continued working, painstakingly removing varnish from the muzzle of the superb bay mare depicted in the painting. When the door behind her opened a few minutes later she glanced round, expecting it to be one of the Mackenzies.

In that first, split second Lynn thought it was *him*. Her heart almost ceased beating. The man was tall and lean-limbed, with dark hair and suntanned skin . . . but he was not Brett Sackville! He was younger by some years and shorter by a couple of inches, slightly thicker set, and the hue of his skin was more olive than brown.

Bowing, the man advanced another step towards her. "I startled you, *señorita*, no? I must make apologies, but Señora Mackenzie told me you were in here, and I came to introduce myself." He drew himself up rather grandly, clicking his heels together and announced, "I am Rafael Alejandro."

While Lynn was still regarding the new arrival dazedly, the housekeeper popped her head round the door.

"This is Don Rafael, Miss Forster," she explained. "You know, Mr. Brett's half-brother that I was telling you about."

"Oh . . . oh yes, of course!" Lynn murmured quickly, holding out her hand to him. "I'm sorry not to have guessed at once who you were, Señor Alejandro."

"Why should you be expected to know me, *señorita*?" he said, dismissing her apology, and before Lynn realised his intention he had taken her hand and raised it to his lips. Never before in her life had a man kissed her hand in such a manner. It was, she discovered, a pleasant experience.

When Mrs. Mackenzie had withdrawn, saying that she would make them some tea, Lynn remarked awkwardly, "Mr. Sackville didn't mention that you were coming, *señor*."

"No, my arrival was unplanned," the young Spaniard told her. "I have been cruising in the West Indies on a friend's yacht. Today we berthed at Southampton, and I thought to myself . . . I shall drop in at *La Casa Española*. Brett might be there as it is the weekend. And if he is not, then I shall stay for one night, and catch a plane home tomorrow."

Already, Lynn had the feeling that she was going to like Rafael Alejandro. He seemed good company, with none of the scorn and arrogance of his English half-brother.

"I expect Mrs. Mackenzie has already explained that Mr. Sackville has just left for Spain."

"*Sí sí, señorita! Dios mío*, he is crazy, that brother of mine. Always, he says the work must be done today! Myself, I ask, what is wrong with *mañana*?"

118

He really had an engaging smile, Lynn decided. In his case, unlike Brett Sackville's, any mockery in his manner was turned upon himself. Yet, to her surprise, she found herself defending Brett.

"I imagine he must have a great deal to do. Sackville Wines are very well-known over here; you see them on sale everywhere." She hesitated. "Your brother seems a young man to be the head of such a sizeable firm."

"But Brett is not young! He is over thirty!"

"Well, I don't call that old!" she riposted.

The Spaniard gave her a quick, shrewd glance. "I think you like my brother, *si*?"

"Heavens, no!" Lynn said emphatically ... much too emphatically, for the expressive eyebrows had shot up even higher. She hastily tried to backpedal. "I mean, the question of my liking Mr. Sackville doesn't arise. I'm not a friend of his. I've been commissioned by him to restore these paintings, that's all."

"*Sí*, Señora Mackenzie explained why you are here. But who else except Brett would fly off to *España* and leave a lovely girl like you to fend for herself in his home?"

"I'm hardly fending for myself," she protested with a laugh. "I'm waited on hand and foot by the Mackenzies."

At that moment, as if in confirmation of Lynn's statement, the housekeeper put her head round the door again to say that tea was ready.

In the lounge, Lynn presided over the teapot while Rafael watched her approvingly, leaning back in an armchair with his neatly trousered legs crossed at the knee.

"This is a good English habit, I think, this tea for two. We can get to know each other."

"I look rather a mess, I'm afraid," Lynn apologised, suddenly conscious of her appearance. "These are my working clothes."

"You look charming!" he assured

her. "I think it is remarkably clever of you to do such skillful work, Lynn . . . I may call you Lynn, *sí*?"

"Of course!" She smiled nervously, feeling oddly shy.

"Thank you! And you must call me Rafael." He took the cup of tea she proferred him, and stirred it absently. "If I were to tell a Spanish girl that she was clever, it would be no compliment. But here in England it is different, no? A young woman is permitted to be both clever *and* beautiful. As you are! Oh, yes, I shall enjoy my stay here."

Lynn met his frankly admiring dark eyes, then looked away in slight confusion. "But you are flying to Spain tomorrow," she reminded him.

"A correction, please!" he said, waving one finger in the air. "I *was* flying to *España* tomorrow. Now I have changed my mind. I shall remain here and keep you company."

She felt a warm little glow of pleasure at the prospect. But at the same time an alarm bell buzzed. Was he getting the wrong idea about her, just as his brother had done? She must be on her guard in case Rafael, too, turned out to be a libertine, intent on making love to every attractive woman he encountered.

And yet, glancing at him covertly from behind the veil of her lashes, she found this hard to believe. His gaze, still fixed upon her, could only be described as one of the purest admiration. For all his obvious wealth and position, there was an endearing quality of boyish enthusiasm about Rafael Alejandro. He was, she felt convinced, the very opposite of a cynic.

"You seem to lead a very easy-going life," she observed. "You're just back from cruising in the West Indies, and now on the spur of the moment you've decided to stay in England for a while. Aren't there any business matters needing your attention in Spain?"

His face lengthened comically. "Ah, now you spoil it for me, Lynn! You sound just like my tyrant brother. But what is the use of having overseers and managers if you do not trust them to do their work? Brett, he trusts nobody!" he added with a shrug.

Yes, that's absolutely true, Lynn thought in the privacy of her mind. *Trust* is a word quite alien to Brett Sackville. He would no doubt consider it ludicrous to place one's implicit trust in another person.

Feeling curious about the relationship between the two brothers, she asked Rafael if their business lives were closely connected. "Mrs. Mackenzie explained to me when I first arrived that your side of the family is also in the wine trade."

He nodded. "But we are growers . . . producers, and the Sackvilles are wine importers. It is part of the history of sherry, Lynn, these close connections between English and Spanish families. After Brett's father died and he inherited the business, his mother married Emilio Alejandro, and . . ." white teeth flashed in a smile, "I am the outcome! Alas, my own father died also, so the Alejandro estates are now in my hands. But although Brett and I are brothers, the business interests remain separate." His handsome, olive-hued face darkened slightly at a disagreeable thought. "Or at least, they are in theory. In practice . . . " He spread his hands expressively.

"What happens in practice?" Lynn probed.

"My father, God rest his soul, had no high opinion of my aptitude for business," Rafael explained ruefully, "and in his will he named Brett as a trustee until I should reach the mature wisdom of twenty-five years. In my father's eyes, Brett was a paragon who could do no wrong."

"I see!"

Lynn's heart went out in sympathy to the charming young man who sat opposite her. To be under the thumb of the arrogant, intolerant, overbearing Brett Sackville seemed a particularly cruel twist of fate. Even if Rafael *was* a little indolent and inclined to take life easy, surely a kinder solution could have been found?

"Never mind," she smiled consolingly. "I don't suppose there's long to go before your twenty-fifth birthday, and then you'll be free to run your own affairs."

He pulled a gloomy face. "Another two years yet! So I still have much solemn lecturing to endure . . . to be told that *this* must be done, and *that* attended to without delay. *Madre de Dios!*" he added with a heartfelt sigh, "Anyone would think that being the owner of one of *España*'s great vineyards would place me in a slightly privileged position. But Brett scorns privilege and talks always of *responsibility!*"

"Your brother can hardly be described as outstandingly responsible in all things," Lynn observed.

Rafael looked at her curiously. "And what is that sly remark intended to convey?"

"Oh . . . nothing!"

"Come now," he pressed her, with a teasing smile. "I think you are not the sort of person to say things for no reason."

"Well, it's only . . . " She hesitated, then went on in a little rush, "He seems to have a rather . . . well, contemptuous attitude towards women."

"To you, you mean?" Rafael asked quickly, sitting up straight in his chair.

"No, of course not!" she insisted falsely. "It's just . . . well, it was an impression I gathered from various things he said, and . . . and the way Señora Vazquez arrived here and the two of them went off together. He seemed to take her very much for granted, I thought."

Rafael relaxed visibly. "Ah so . . . the formidable Doña Juanita! She sought Brett out here at *La Casa Española*, did she? You have too soft a heart, Lynn. There is no more determined woman in the world than Juanita Vazquez. You need not waste your sympathy on her."

In the days that followed, Lynn had to admit that having Rafael around added greatly to life's enjoyment. He was wonderfully entertaining and every mealtime became a pleasurable occasion instead of the torment it had been in his brother's company. Whenever Rafael spoke of his homeland, which was often, his velvet-soft eyes grew dreamy and his voice was husky with affection.

"I cannot bear to be away from *España* for long," he confessed to Lynn one evening after dinner, as they strolled in the shadowed dusk of the scented garden.

"You could go back tomorrow, if you wanted to!" Lynn reminded him with a matter-of-factness she didn't feel.

He paused on the stone-flagged path, and she paused too.

"You know why I stay here, Lynn," he murmured softly.

"Do I?" she parried.

"Of course you do! I only had to take one look at you, the day I arrived, and I knew . . . I knew in those first moments, that you were a girl I could easily fall in love with."

Lynn felt her heart begin to thud, and she tried to calm it.

"Really, Rafael!" she protested with a little laugh. "There's no need to exaggerate like that."

"I do not exaggerate!" he said almost fiercely. "I speak the simple truth. Do you not feel something for *me*, Lynn *cara*? Just a little!"

"Of course I do. I . . . I'm growing very fond of you. But . . . but not . . . "

Suddenly his arms were about her, and she felt his strength as he grasped her. His lips brushed against her hair, and he began murmuring soft endearments in his own tongue which she could not understand.

"No, Rafael, you mustn't!" she protested, straining away from him. But he held her close, and she was powerless to free herself.

"*Sí sí!*" he whispered ardently. "Do not fight against your feelings,

Lynn . . . do not be afraid because it is so soon. This is how I have always believed love must happen . . . suddenly, without warning. I adore you, *querida*! Please . . . please tell me that you return my love."

She raised her head to look at him and in the glow of lamplight spilling from the house she was able to discern his eyes, glittering with ardour. His lips were parted, so that she felt his warm breath upon her brow.

"Rafael, listen to me!" she began nervously. "You must understand . . . "

Lynn could say no more, because Rafael was kissing her; his lips soft and beseeching, not hard and demanding as Brett's had been. She felt no need to turn in panic and flee, as she had done on that other occasion with his brother, but she knew that she had no future in his arms and that she must escape him.

"Oh Lynn!" he murmured on a breath. "*Cara mía!*"

Every second that she remained in

Rafael's arms, accepting his ardent kisses, his softly whispered words of adoration, she was misleading him. She was using Rafael as Brett Sackville had used her — selfishly, for personal esteem only, without thought for the feelings of the other person involved.

"Rafael!" she begged weakly. "Please . . . please listen to me! I am fond of you, yes — but I do not love you."

His breath was fast and shallow. "Not yet, perhaps, *amada*, but soon . . . soon you will come to love me as deeply as I love you."

"No . . . no, it isn't possible!"

He still held her but thrust away from him now, jealously searching her eyes.

"Why not, Lynn? Is there another man? Tell me!"

"No, it's not that!" Then realising this wasn't wholly true, she amended carefully, "No, it isn't because I'm in love with somebody else, Rafael."

Her words seemed to satisfy him. Smiling he kissed her once more, chastely upon the brow, then let her go.

"As long as I have no rival in your affections, *cara mia*, then I will *make* you love me. You will see!"

★ ★ ★

Rafael spent hours of each day in Lynn's 'studio,' watching her as she worked. To her surprise she could concentrate with him there, and the work went quickly. Soon she would be finished, free to leave *La Casa Española* and still, as he had threatened, Brett had not returned.

Lynn took care to avoid giving Rafael the impression that her feelings for him were changing. She was consistently friendly, but no more than that. Whenever she scented danger from an intimate turn in the conversation, she steered it into a safer channel. As a consequence, they often fell to discussing the work she was doing.

"One can never hope to restore a

work of art to its original condition," she explained one day. "In America, picture restorers are more often called 'conservators,' and really that makes more sense. Paintings inevitably deteriorate with the passing of time, and all we can do is delay the process."

"I believe I read somewhere that it is even possible to replace the very canvas on which a picture is painted."

"Yes, that's true," she said. "There are a great many things that can be done — the only thing we can't do is to try and improve upon the artist's inspiration. It's this that *makes* a work of art, and no restorer — no *ethical* restorer — would ever attempt to interfere." She smiled apologetically. "Oh dear, I'm getting on my hobby-horse!"

"Hobby-horse! What is this?"

"Well, my special interest . . . I could go on about it for hours. Like you could, I expect, about the making of wine."

He shrugged dismissively. "That

would be boring."

"Oh no! I think it's terribly romantic the way an ancient skill has been handed down over the centuries. You must tell me how sherry is made, I'm completely ignorant about it."

"One day, perhaps, when you are in *España*."

Rafael went to the window and stood staring out at the garden. A fine drizzle was falling today, and there was a distinct chill in the air. He was silent for so long that Lynn resumed her work at the easel. But she felt somehow uneasy, without knowing why.

At length he turned back and began tentatively, "Lynn, I have been considering . . . you tell me you are almost done here. When you have finished, why not come to *España* with me?"

In her astonishment, Lynn dropped the cotton wool swab she was holding onto the floor.

"But Rafael, I . . . I thought I'd made you understand that there can be nothing between us — nothing beyond friendship."

He gave her a faint, wary smile. "I would not ask you to come on any other terms," he said earnestly, "but I make no secret that I go on hoping. If we can be together, I feel confident that soon you will begin to feel for me something of what I feel for you."

"No . . . no, it's impossible!"

"Let me be the judge of that, Lynn," he begged. "Please say you will come to *España* and stay at my house. It will be quite proper" he added quickly. "My mother is there, and there are many servants, so we shall not be alone. You will come, yes Lynn?"

"No, of course I won't! It — it's out of the question. Besides, I have my living to earn. You seem to forget that, Rafael."

He was immediately triumphant.

"I have not forgotten, I have remembered it very well! That is what makes my plan so perfect, Lynn. You see, at *La Casa de los Pámpanos* there are many paintings which need restoring . . . "

He broke off, seeing the flash of anger in Lynn's eyes. She felt bitterly disappointed in Rafael. His smoke-screen offer of a job for her might be good enough to deceive his mother, but did he imagine that she herself was so innocent and unworldly as to be taken in by it? No longer could she believe his earnest protestations that he truly loved her. It looked now as though, once he had gotten her away from England and staying at his home in Spain, Rafael's intentions would be no more honourable than those of his brother.

"Let's get this straight once and for all, Rafael," she said in a firm cold voice. "I am *not* coming to Spain with you — because there is no good reason why I should. As for pretending that you want me there to restore some paintings, it's insulting to me, and . . . "

Her voice trailed off at Rafael's

genuine look of distress.

"But it is true what I say, Lynn," he protested. "You must believe me! At *Los Pámpanos* there are many old paintings — some of them quite valuable, I believe — which are grown dingy and dark, just like these of Brett's were before you restored them. I swear to you it is true . . . there really is work for you to do there, *cara*."

"Why have you never asked to have the paintings restored before?" she asked, her suspicions lulled, but still not laid to rest.

"Because the idea never before occurred to me. But having seen the wonderful way you have transformed these paintings here, I am eager for you to do the same with the ones in my home."

He seemed so utterly sincere that Lynn couldn't go on mistrusting him. She said, more gently now,

"Well, I accept what you say, Rafael, but it makes no difference. I'm still not coming. There are picture restorers in

Spain, too, so you'll be able to get someone."

"But I want *you*, Lynn," he pleaded. "Please do not refuse."

"I'm sorry, but I must!"

He threw up his hands in an expression of despair. "Then I shall remain here with you."

"But you can't, Rafael — don't be silly. As soon as I've finished this job, I shall be returning to my flat in London."

"I shall go to London too!" he said obstinately. "I shall see you all the time, *cara*, and one day you will find that you love me, after all. And we shall be happy together."

"No, Rafael!" she protested, dismayed at the prospect that this determined young man would pursue her wherever she went. "You must not follow me to London."

"Then come to *España* with me. You will adore it, *amada*, it is all so beautiful. Come and spend the summer at *Los Pámpanos* and put my paintings in good order. Then if you are still determined not to love me, I will let you go. I give you my word."

Lynn hesitated. She was surprised at how strongly tempted she felt. Rafael was offering her commissioned work in her own profession, which was something she would badly need when her present job for Brett Sackville came to an end. She had already made it clear to Rafael that he must never expect her to return his love, that going to Spain with him wouldn't make any difference to her feelings. So there seemed no good reason why she shouldn't accept his offer with a clear conscience.

"Very well then, Rafael," she consented. "As soon as I have finished here, I'll come to Spain and examine your paintings. But I shall only remain if I'm satisfied that some of them genuinely need restoring, and that I can do what is required. Otherwise, I shall return to England at once. Is that agreed?"

His dark eyes shone with delight.

"Oh, my wonderful Lynn, I am so happy! If nothing else will keep you in my country, the blue skies of Andalusia will make you want to stay there forever."

The blue skies of Andalusia! And somewhere under them was a man named Brett Sackville. Would he be at *La Casa de los Pámpanos* when she arrived, Lynn wondered with a little shiver of apprehension. And if so, how would he greet her?

# 5

AS Lynn, with Rafael beside her at the wheel of his powerful sports car, was whisked along the dusty Spanish road, the afternoon sun blazed down from a clear blue sky, the very air glowing with a kind of crystal translucence. It was all such a contrast, she thought blissfully, to the succession of grey wet days that seemed to have tormented England recently.

They were among vineyards now, Alejandro vineyards, Rafael told her with pride. Serried ranks of dark-leaved vines, their tight bunches of grapes already formed but as yet small and unripe, rolled away into the distance where Lynn had glimpses of the shimmering, silver-gilt sea. Groups of peasant women dressed in full black skirts and wide-brimmed straw hats were hoeing among the vines. They paused to watch with impassive eyes as the car went by, and Rafael gave them a cheery wave of greeting. Further on, at a point where the land rose from the road in steep terraces, a group of men was hard at work shovelling earth, raising a cloud of thick red dust. Rafael slowed the car, looking puzzled.

"There appears to be something wrong, Lynn. I'd better go and see what's happening. I won't be long."

Getting out, he started to climb up the bank towards the workmen who by now had paused in their labours, wiping sweaty brows and easing aching backs. One of them detached himself from the rest and clambered down to meet Rafael. Something about the way he moved caught Lynn's attention, something familiar . . . though like all the others he was caked in dust from head to toe. As he and Rafael met, the man lifted his chin belligerently, and in that instant Lynn recognised him. It was Brett!

So the question she'd asked herself

a hundred times since agreeing to come to Spain had been answered. But what Brett was doing labouring among the peasants she couldn't begin to understand. It seemed so extraordinary, so out of character for the immaculate man she'd known in England.

Brett was angry, that much was plain from the tone of his raised voice. As he and Rafael turned and walked in the direction of the car, Lynn began to pick out his actual words. It was obvious that he didn't yet realise she was here, and she steeled herself for his discovery of that fact.

"It's just about the limit, Rafael," he was saying vehemently. "When I arrived here and heard you suddenly decided to go off cruising in the Carribean, I thought that was bad enough! But you were due back from the cruise over a week ago. Where the hell have you been since?"

Rafael muttered a reply, and his half-brother stormed on, "But your place is *here*! When will you learn to accept your responsibilities? Hundreds of people depend on this estate for their livelihood, and without proper supervision from the owner, the place will run to rack and ruin. This trouble today is just one example of the shocking way you've been neglecting things . . . "

The two men were close to the car now and noticing someone sitting inside, Brett turned his head to look. Lynn saw recognition dawn in his eyes, before they narrowed in swift anger.

"What in the name of heaven are you doing here?" he rapped.

"I . . . I came with Rafael . . . " she faltered.

"I can see that for myself, Miss Forster!" he said bitingly. As if she were not worth wasting words on, he turned on Rafael again. "What the devil have you brought the girl here for?"

Already, to her consternation, Lynn had noticed how cowed Rafael had become in the face of his elder brother's wrath. Now it was even worse, and he stuttered as he tried to explain the situation.

"You see, Brett, I . . . I happened to drop in at *La Casa Española*, hoping you would be there. Instead, I found Lynn — er, Señorita Forster, restoring those horse paintings of yours. When I saw the wonderful work she was doing, I thought what a marvellous idea it would be if she came and did the same here. There are dozens of paintings that need attention. So I . . . I persuaded her to come with me."

"I can imagine," Brett said sarcastically, "that she didn't require much in the way of persuasion. Eh, Miss Forster? Or was it you who first put the idea in my brother's mind? I wouldn't put it past you!"

"I did nothing of the kind!" she retorted indignantly.

"No, honestly Brett," Rafael intervened. "It . . . it was entirely my own idea. As a matter of fact, it took me quite a while to talk her into it."

"I don't care a damn which way round it was!" Brett snapped at his brother, and Lynn detected a new, steely edge to his voice. "When are you going to grow up, for God's sake? When are you going to learn to give a lead to your employees?" The begrimed, sweat-soaked shirt he wore was stuck to his skin and he tugged it away from his shoulders impatiently. "Look Rafael, there's an urgent job to be done right here — now — and it's one of those times when the only decent thing for a boss to do is to roll up his sleeves and work alongside the men, and not care about getting his hands dirty! So take that girl up to the house and then get back here as fast as you can. Understand?"

He turned away without giving Lynn so much as another glance. As Rafael drove on, tight-lipped and silent beside her, Lynn wished desperately that she had never agreed to come to Spain. The hot sun, which a few minutes ago had seemed so benevolent, now beat down with a harsh, pitiless glare. She just wanted to find a dark corner somewhere, and hide in it.

They came upon *La Casa do los Pámpanos* quite suddenly. Lynn, still dazed from their encounter with Brett, gained a confused impression of a stately building that, in this fierce light, gleamed ten times whiter than The Spanish House in Sussex. The rooftiles were a deep rich terra-cotta, baked by the heat of a hundred southern summers. Each window, balconied with a delicate grillwork of iron, presented a blind eye to the world, shielded by green-painted shutters.

Rafael stopped the car before a flight of wide, shallow steps that led up to the front entrance.

"Lynn," he began apologetically, "I deeply regret what happened back there. *Dios mío*, Brett has a cruel tongue! I am his brother, so it does not matter what he says to me, but he has no right to speak to you as he did."

"Don't worry about it, Rafael, I shan't," she responded with a brave, shaky smile. "Anyhow, what was he so steamed up about?"

"Oh, it is a — how do you say? — a retaining wall that is breaking away. Brett says there is fear of a dangerous landslide if it is not put right at once."

"Even so, I don't see that there was any cause for him to get so nasty about it. After all, you couldn't have known such a thing was going to happen."

He flashed her a grateful smile. "You are very sweet, Lynn *cara*. Now, if you will excuse me, I shall escort you inside and ensure that you are well looked after. The servants will bring anything you require, you have only to ask. As for myself, I had better do what that brother of mine says, or he will only become still more angry."

A few minutes later, Lynn was being led up a grand marble staircase by a shy little raven-haired maid, who showed her into one of the *casa*'s guest rooms.

Lynn hardly bothered to take note of her luxurious surroundings, just sinking thankfully onto the bed the moment she was alone. For a long while she lay there unmoving, staring up at the lofty, shadowed ceiling, still feeling badly shaken by that encounter with Brett Sackville.

Of course it was wrong of Rafael to neglect his responsibilities at the vineyard, and she appreciated that Brett did have an interest in the matter, having been appointed trustee by his stepfather until Rafael's twenty-fifth birthday. But that hardly gave him an excuse for behaving like a truculent bully! After all, how would Brett like it if the tables were turned and Rafael had the right to interfere in the running of Sackville Wines in England? She could only suppose that having such power and authority over his younger brother had gone to Brett's head. It fit the character of the man as she had observed it. Didn't he similarly delight in his power over women, making them vulnerable and toying with their emotions for his own amusement?

The young maid came tapping at the door, bringing the tea that Lynn had asked for. She drank it gratefully, finding that it refreshed her dry, burning throat. Then, exhausted by the day's events and the unaccustomed heat, she slipped into a state of limbo, somewhere between waking and sleeping. Yet all the while, rising sharply etched from the swirling mist of her thoughts, was the aggressive figure of Brett Sackville as she had last seen him — his shirt begrimed and clinging to his body from the sweat of manual labour, his dark eyes, rimmed with the red dust of the fields, glaring at her angrily with unconcealed contempt.

Somehow, she had to find the courage to face him again.

★ ★ ★

She was roused by the same young maid with a message that dinner would be served in less than an hour's time. Heavy with fatigue, Lynn dragged herself off the bed. It had grown dark outside and the maid switched on subdued lighting and drew the curtains across the windows, then enquired if she should run Lynn a bath.

"*Muchas gracias*, that would be nice."

Fully awake now, Lynn gave her attention to the accommodation she'd been allotted, surveying the room with wondering eyes. It was by far the largest bedroom she had ever occupied in her life and furnished in a luxurious blend of period charm and modern amenities, evidenced by the springy mattress on the vast, ornately-carved bed, and the up-to-the-minute bathroom, oyster-pink with black and white tiling, which she could glimpse through the open door. The bedroom walls were hung with silk flocked paper in shades of rich cream, and the full-length drapes were of heavy, satiny material. The floor was uncarpeted — clearly for the sake of coolness — but covered with smooth, polished tiles and colourful scatter rugs.

She wondered bleakly how long she'd be staying here ... how long she *could* stay here now. Brett Sackville would see to it that things were made impossible for her, setting his mother against her and browbeating Rafael to such an extent that she would have no ally there. Still, as long as she *did* remain, she would behave with dignity and not allow Brett to gloat over his triumph.

After a bath in silky, scented water that did much to revive her, Lynn pondered carefully on what she should wear. Finally, she chose the long blue and white dress of uncrushable crepe. It was lightweight enough to be comfortable, the evening was still very warm even though the sun had set some time ago, and with its high neckline and soft full folds it was demure enough to satisfy whatever Spanish proprieties had infiltrated this semi-English household.

Giving her appearance a final check in a full-length cheval glass, she left the room and walked to the head of the grand staircase.

There was no one about as she slowly descended, one hand on the elegant carved balustrade, the other holding up her skirt, and she wondered if perhaps she should have waited in her room until she was summoned. But, as she reached the marble-pillared hall, a white-jacketed manservant glided forward and ushered her deferentially through double doors into a large apartment which glittered brightly with the light from a pair of ornate chandeliers. To her relief, Brett wasn't there but Rafael was, together with a silver-haired woman whom she knew from the photograph at The Spanish House to be the mother of the two men.

As Rafael came towards her, his eyes were sparkling, and Lynn realised thankfully that his brother had not succeeded in crushing him completely.

"Lynn, come and meet my mother," he said eagerly. "I have been telling her all about you . . . how clever you are at the fascinating work you do, and she is eager to hear more about it."

He led her across to where Señora Alejandro was seated gracefully upon a crimson brocade sofa. There was a definite elegance about the older woman, but no sign of haughtiness. The smile she gave Lynn as they were presented to one another was charming and altogether friendly. So her elder son had not yet had the opportunity of sowing distrust in her mind, Lynn thought! That was something to be grateful for.

"My dear Miss Forster, I am so pleased to meet you!" The voice was pleasantly modulated, but somewhat frail. This, together with her pale complexion, reminded Lynn of something Mrs. Mackenzie had said . . . that Brett's mother's health wasn't all that it might be.

"Good evening, Señora Alejandro,"

she replied, smiling in response. "What a beautiful home you have!"

Faded eyes sparked with pleasure. "Thank you, my dear. Come, sit here beside me and join us in an aperitif. Will a glass of our own *manzanilla* suit your taste? Or would you prefer something different?"

"I should very much like to try some of your own wine," said Lynn, sitting down.

"Good! Now you must tell me how you came to take up such an unusual profession as picture restoration."

Lynn explained that she had been trained by her father and that, now that he was dead, she was hoping to continue the business he had created.

"Excellent! I deeply approve of maintaining family tradition. Each of my two sons is carrying on a family concern bequeathed to him by his father — Brett in England, and Rafael here in Spain. Of course," she added, with a roguish pursing of her lips, "this younger boy of mine still needs a guiding hand. It's fortunate, isn't it Rafael, that Brett is prepared to give so much of his time to keeping an eye on things here?"

Covertly, Rafael pulled a wry face at Lynn. "I suppose so, *Madre*," he replied with a heartfelt sigh. "But I do wish that Brett didn't always get so hot and bothered about every slightest thing that goes wrong. We do not do things that way here in *España*!"

"Then it's about time you started to!" clipped a dry, hard voice from the doorway, and they all turned to see Brett entering.

Every trace of the grime that had smothered him was gone now. He looked immaculate in a white dinner jacket, with navy blue trousers, and his springy dark hair was clean and gleaming. Ignoring Lynn, he stood regarding his half-brother critically.

"In actual fact, Rafael, you're quite wrong though," he went on. "The Spanish are just as hardworking as any other nationality, only they don't make such a public show of efficiency. So it's no use you hiding behind this *mañana* myth as an excuse for not getting things done."

Rafael looked a little abashed, but clearly his earlier fear of his brother had evaporated now that Brett's fierce outburst of temper was over.

"Oh, do have a drink, Brett, and stop lecturing me," he said with a boyishly rueful grin.

Brett took a quick breath, as if caught on the raw again. But his mother intervened smoothly between her two sons — perhaps something she was well-accustomed to doing.

"Miss Forster was just telling us about her work, Brett. I understand from Rafael that she has restored the horse paintings at *La Casa Española* most beautifully."

The slate-grey eyes were impenetrable. "Perhaps Rafael is prejudiced in Miss Forster's favour, Mother. Since I was not there to see the pictures finished,

I am in no position to pass judgment on her work."

His mother gave him a reproving glance. "Don't be so unchivalrous, Brett! You would not have commissioned the young lady if you didn't have every confidence in her ability."

Brett shrugged, and crossed to a gilded console table standing against the wall to pour himself a glass of sherry.

"For the sake of accuracy, Miss Forster, should we not put the record straight?" he said over his shoulder. "I didn't commission *you*, did I? I expected your father."

Lynn was taken aback, but she quickly recovered her poise.

"In my profession, Mr. Sackville, and presumably in all other forms of artistic work, people expect to be judged purely on ability — not on age or sex."

Before he could answer, his mother interposed smoothly, "I feel very proud of the young women of my own nationality who are no longer content to leave all professional endeavours to men. Things are also changing here in Spain, but not so rapidly as in England."

"A Spanish woman knows that it is enough for her purpose to be beautiful and agreeable," her elder son observed. "To confront a man with cleverness, too, may be a positive disadvantage."

"Are you afraid of clever women, Mr. Sackville?" Lynn dared to challenge him.

With a look that was meant to shrivel her, he rejoined, "*Afraid* is not quite the word I should use, Miss Forster."

She hated to have him score against her so easily, and would dearly have liked to strike back. But her position here hardly permitted her to cross swords with a member of the family. Besides, she had no wish to antagonise Señora Alejandro. So she kept silent, taking another sip from her glass.

Mercifully, the dignified butler appeared just at that moment to announce dinner.

Although there were only four of them, the meal was served in a grand, ornate dining-room at a table long enough to seat a dozen or more. Rafael, theoretically the master of the house, took his place at the head of the table, with his mother at the other end. Thus, to Lynn's embarrassment, she found herself placed nearer to Brett than to either of the other two, being separated from him merely by the width of the table.

The meal began with wafer-thin slices of mountain ham served with chilled melon. Lynn discovered that she had quite an appetite despite the man sitting opposite her, the man whose dark eyes she could feel upon her the whole time, so that it was imperative not to glance in his direction. This *hors d'oeuvre* was followed by a dish of roast tuna steak with a delicious tomato sauce, flavoured with herbs.

The conversation turned to places of interest in Andalusia, and Señora

159

Alejandro mentioned the eighth-century mosque at Cordoba. Rafael pounced on this excitedly.

"I will take you there, Lynn . . . it is a fantastic place to see. There are hundreds and hundreds of Moorish arches supported on columns of onyx and jasper and marble — all the colours of the rainbow! It is truly magnificent! Oh, and there is so much else I must show you . . . the Alhambra at Granada, and the little town of Arcos de la Frontera perched up on a rocky crag, and the Aracena grotto, and . . . and Cádiz, and the cathedral at Seville and so many other marvellous sights. You're going to fall in love with Andalusia, just as I said you would! To me, it is the most wonderful place on earth, and I am so eager for you to think the same . . . "

Rafael broke off abruptly, realising that he'd let his enthusiasm run away with his tongue. There was an awkward silence around the table, and Señora Alejandro shot a look in

Lynn's direction that was a mixture of speculation and anxiety. Up until now, she had apparently accepted without question her younger son's version of the reason for Lynn's presence. But now, without doubt, she was having second thoughts. She couldn't have failed to notice the look of adoration on Rafael's face as he had been enthusing to Lynn about the beauties of his country.

Acutely embarrassed, Lynn knew that she must try her best to put things right. Carefully averting her eyes from Brett to avoid meeting his scornful gaze, she said quickly,

"It's very kind of you, Rafael, to offer to show me around, but I honestly don't think I'll have any time for sightseeing. You see, if I do decide to stay here for a while and work on your paintings, I shall be kept pretty busy. But thanks all the same."

Rafael looked downcast, but Lynn could tell at once that she had allayed his mother's fears. As the older woman glanced at her, smiling faintly, Lynn detected a message of gratitude beneath her tranquil expression.

"You will be busy yourself, Rafael dear," she said gently. "According to Brett, there is a lot of work needing your attention on the estate." She looked at her other son enquiringly. "I gather from something my maid Luzia mentioned that the retaining wall you were repairing this afternoon was in imminent danger of collapse. Is this true?"

Brett's face darkened. "That wall has been in imminent danger of collapse ever since Manuel first warned Rafael months ago that the winter rains had undermined it. This morning, Manuel came running to me in a panic to say that the cracks were opening up. If the wall had suddenly given way, his cottage would have been engulfed, perhaps his wife and children, too!"

"*Por Dios!*" protested Rafael, looking uncomfortable. "You exaggerate, Brett! It wasn't as bad as that."

"How do you know, when you weren't on the spot?" said Brett bitterly. "The work of shoring up the earth was almost completed when you turned up."

"Is it my fault the job was neglected?" Rafael grumbled sulkily. "What was the foreman doing, not to have seen to the matter long ago?"

"It's no good you trying to pass the buck," Brett snapped back, his patience fraying again. "Being the owner of an estate like this doesn't mean just sitting back and enjoying the fruits of other men's labours. You've got to be the one to give them a lead, Rafael."

His brother's face had turned a bright red. The Señora gave Brett a reproachful shake of her head. "I think the dinner table is hardly the place for discussing business, Brett dear. Besides, you are forgetting we have a guest. You are embarrassing Miss Forster."

Instantly his gaze fastened on Lynn, stinging her with its intensity. She felt herself trembling inwardly, wondering

163

what scathing remark he was about to make. But after a moment's hesitation, he shrugged and reached for his wineglass.

"You are right, Mother, and I apologise. Miss Forster must not be involved in matters which are the private concern of the family. They are nothing whatever to do with her."

What sort of apology was that? Lynn wondered miserably — words chosen for the purpose of humiliating her. But Señora Alejandro seemed to notice nothing untoward in her son's remark. She was too intent on making a hidden point herself.

"I hope, Rafael," she began, as if at a sudden thought, "that you will telephone Rosa-María tomorrow morning. The poor girl has been quite desolate without you. I have invited her here a few times while you were away, but what company is an elderly invalid for a pretty young girl? Wouldn't it be delightful," she ran on eagerly, "if we were able to announce your betrothal very soon? You have kept Rosa-María waiting long enough."

Startled, Lynn glanced at Rafael. Nothing in his attitude towards her, since they first met at *La Casa Española* back in England, had given her the slightest clue that he had a girlfriend in Spain . . . a serious girlfriend, whom his mother clearly believed he was intending to marry. Fleetingly, Rafael met Lynn's questioning gaze and gave a tiny shake of his head, as if denying everything.

"Oh *Madre*!" he protested. "Rosa-María is a sweet girl, but she is only a child."

"She is nineteen years of age, my son! And she loves you devotedly." Rafael's mother broke off and glanced apologetically at Lynn. "Now I am the one at fault, Miss Forster. All this must be so boring to you."

"Not at all!" Lynn murmured faintly.

"Whatever else our guest might be, Mother," put in Brett ironically, "you can be assured she is not bored. She once confessed to me that at heart she is a romantic. If that is true, then news of an engagement in the air will . . . will catch her imagination. Isn't that so, Miss Forster?"

"There is *no* engagement in the air!" Rafael interjected fiercely. "Brett, I wish to heaven that you and *Madre* would not try and join my name with Rosa-María's."

"But Rafael dear," his mother rebuked him, "I thought you were so fond of the dear girl."

"I *am* fond of her," Rafael acknowledged, straining to keep his temper. "But not — not to the extent that I wish to marry her."

"You mean you are not quite ready for marriage yet?" queried Señora Alejandro, regarding him with troubled eyes. "You want to give it a little more time, is that it, Rafael?"

He flicked a helpless glance at Lynn, as if asking her pardon for something. "Oh *Madre*!" he muttered wretchedly, his voice scarcely audible. "You do not understand!"

There was silence around the table, and the feeling of tension in the air was so tangible that Lynn wished to heaven that someone would speak. At length, Señora Alejandro gave a long, heavy sigh, and remarked,

"You seem to have changed greatly in the short time you have been away, Rafael. It almost makes me wonder if . . . if . . . "

Rafael's mother knew — there was no doubt about it — that he was in love with her, Lynn realised. Though she'd already tried to make it clear to Señora Alejandro that she didn't reciprocate his feelings, it looked as though she must redouble her efforts if she were to completely reassure the older woman.

To the table at large, she said brightly, "I am so anxious to see the paintings which you think are in need of restoration. Of course, I require daylight to give them a proper examination, but would it perhaps be possible for me to have a preliminary look at them this evening?"

Too late, she realised her ploy was also handing Rafael an opportunity to be alone with her, and he jumped at it eagerly.

"Yes Lynn, of course! As soon as we have finished dinner I shall give you a conducted tour."

"No, that will not do at all, Rafael," his mother interposed quickly. Then realising how sharply she had spoken she went on in a gentler tone, "I meant, of course, that you know so little about the family art collection. I think it would be more suitable if *I* showed Miss Forster round."

Rafael was clearly about to argue the point, but another voice, speaking with utter firmness and decision, stopped him openmouthed.

"No Mother," Brett insisted, "it is not right for you to be traipsing around the house at an hour when you should have retired for the night. I shall take

Miss Forster myself. That, I think, is the best way for her to gain a clear and concise indication of what we require from her."

★ ★ ★

Brett led the way into a huge, gloomy salon, switching on only a single shaded wall sconce so that the farther reaches of the room were lost in shadow. Closing the double doors carefully, he stood with his back to them.

Lynn waited on shaking legs, scared of his anger, scared of the cruel lash of his tongue. He stood looking at her for long seconds in silence . . . keeping her in suspense, deliberately building up her fear of him. She felt like a small trapped animal, remembering how cowed and helpless Rafael had been during their encounter on the road this afternoon. If this man could so easily dominate his younger brother, his equal in terms of money and position in the world, it was little wonder that he could reduce

169

her to this sorry state.

When at last he spoke, his voice sounded hollow in the cavernous room.

"Well, Miss Forster . . . ?"

Somehow Lynn summoned up the last tattered shreds of her courage.

"Well, Mr. Sackville, where are these paintings I'm supposed to be looking at?"

"Oh, for heaven's sake!" he exclaimed with a look of sheer disgust. "Are you going to keep up this ridiculous charade?"

"Ridiculous charade? I . . . I don't understand what you mean."

"How innocent you sound when you try!" he said witheringly. "Miss Forster, would I be simply wasting my time if I asked you to remove your hooks from Rafael? He is young and highly impressionable, no match for a woman of your sort."

"A . . . a woman of my sort!" she gasped, echoing him a second time. "You make me sound like some vile and unspeakable adventuress."

"Your description, not mine!" he said dryly. "Come now, can't we be honest with one another behind these closed doors? There is no one to overhear. Admit to me that in Rafael you see the finest marriage prospect ever to cross your path. It must have seemed a stroke of incredibly good fortune when he turned up at *La Casa Española* just when you'd been forced to relinquish all hope of landing me in your net. I can guess how you were picturing yourself, installed here at *Los Pámpanos* and playing the grand *Señora*, before you had even set eyes on the place. Rafael's wealth must have seemed wonderful beyond anything you'd ever dreamed of."

"That's a despicable thing to say," she cried in a strangled voice.

"It's a despicable thing to do!"

In this dim light his eyes were dark shadowed pools from which Lynn caught a glint of cold condemnation. She wanted to shout at him, somehow make him understand the truth, to justify herself. But her voice, when it emerged, was thin and cracked.

"You are wrong . . . dreadfully wrong! Such thoughts never even entered my head. How could they, when Rafael hasn't properly come into his inheritance yet . . . not for another two years."

"So you had that all worked out too! I've no doubt you judged it worthwhile risking my anger. Two years isn't very long to wait, is it Miss Forster . . . that would be how your scheming mind calculated. Two years of accepting my trusteeship over Rafael, and then . . . how you would have enjoyed helping him squander his fortune."

"Stop it!" she cried. "You're distorting everything in the most horrible way. I . . . I told Rafael quite definitely that I would never be able to love him . . . that if I agreed to come out to Spain with him, it could only be to give an opinion on restoring some of the oil paintings here. Nothing more."

"So you don't deny that you and he talked of love? And *made* love perhaps, in *my* home?" he added savagely.

"No, we didn't . . . we didn't!"

"Not even so much as a kiss?" Brett demanded inexorably.

Cornered, Lynn stared at him in dismay. Then slowly she turned her face away, her eyes downcast. She heard his breath rasp in angry satisfaction at having caught her out.

"Yes, of course . . . you *would* allow a kiss, and nothing more! That age-old feminine trick of advance and retreat, bringing a man to the peak of desire and then tantalisingly stepping back out of reach, so he is left in a state of frustration that's beyond all sense and reason . . . mere putty in your hands."

"No, no; it wasn't like that!" she protested. "When . . . when Rafael kissed me, it meant absolutely nothing to me."

"I'm only surprised that you should admit it, because it just proves my point! I wonder when, if ever, a man's kiss has caused so much as a ripple of excitement to disturb your coldly calculating thoughts."

At bay, Lynn impatiently brushed aside the tears that filled her eyes and hit back wildly.

"And when, to you, has a kiss meant anything more than the gratification of sheer desire?"

"It would take a lot more than a kiss to do that, Miss Forster!" he jeered.

Always, *always* he defeated her. She had to restrain herself from rushing forward and pummelling his chest with her fists, to *make* him end this torture. How *dare* he sneer at her for being cold and calculating, when he knew without a shadow of doubt that his own kiss had left her weak and trembling, fired with an intensity of longing such as she had never experienced before? He knew perfectly well that on that fateful evening on the patio at *La Casa Expañola* she had been poised on the very precipice of surrender, her own soaring desire no less than his.

The need for restraint caused her breast to heave, and the breath caught in her throat. Then, very carefully, in a voice that sounded like a stranger's, she said coolly, "Mr. Sackville, do you intend to show me the paintings I am supposed to be examining? Or are you telling me that you want me to return to England at once?"

"And have Rafael pursue you there? No, Miss Forster, I'm not handing you such a bonus. You will remain here for the time being, so that my brother has a chance to get over his infatuation."

"You can't make me stay if I don't want to," she flung at him.

"Oh, but I can! Imagine what would happen to that precious professional reputation you're so anxious to acquire, if it became known that Miss Lynn Forster, on one of her very first commissions, had ducked out of her obligations without an adequate reason. You see, I would make it my business to circulate the story."

"But I . . . I've not been commissioned yet," she faltered. "Nothing has been settled."

"You gave my brother a promise to examine the paintings and carry out any restoration work you judged necessary," he pointed out. "Are you now saying you would be prepared to give a false opinion, just to provide you with an excuse to leave Spain? Where is the professional integrity in that, Miss Forster?"

"Oh, very well then," she cried. "I'll stay, if you really want me to."

"I *insist* that you stay!" he replied pitilessly. "For the very good reason that while you are here I can keep a close watch on your activities apropos my younger brother. Rafael is impetuous and weakwilled, as you very well know, and I won't stand by and see him destroyed by a woman like you. You may be interested to know that until you bewitched him, he was perfectly happy with the prospect of courting Rosa-María Gomez, who is the daughter of the manager of my shipping office in Cádiz."

Goaded beyond bearing, Lynn burst out on a sob, "So that's what it's all about! All this highflown talk about protecting Rafael from himself is really just to keep your two firms neatly linked together. I suppose that way you'll still have a big say in the running of the Alejandro estate when your trusteeship comes to an end."

A hand shot out and gripped her wrist in a circlet of steel.

"How dare you accuse me of nepotism! Marriage to Rosa-María would be just about the best thing that could happen to Rafael, and I intend it to work out that way."

"You'd be advised to stop interfering and leave Rafael to choose for himself whom he'll marry," she cried, trying to snatch back her hand. "You seem to want to play the role of God, Mr. Sackville — you forget you're only a man!"

Brett's grip on her wrist tightened

until her whole arm felt scorched with pain and it was all she could do not to cry out. His breath was rasping in his throat, and his dark eyes glittered from their pools of shadow.

"You never allow me to forget that I'm a man, Miss Forster . . . and that you are a woman! That's your stock in trade, isn't it — to make sure that every man you meet is kept disturbingly aware of that fact?"

Giving a sudden twist that almost seemed to jerk her arm from her body, Lynn found she was free of him. He still stood between her and the doorway, though, and as she tried to push past him to freedom he caught her again, this time with both arms around her, pinning her against his iron-hard masculinity. In vain, Lynn struggled desperately until he brought his lips down upon hers in a bruising, crushing kiss. Then, hating herself, despising the treacherous weakness that vanquished her will to resist, she yielded to him, her whole being charged with a burning need for fulfilment. Her body arched and moulded itself to his; her lips parted softly before the urgent demand of his lips, and her arms slid up and around his neck.

Lynn lost all consciousness of time and place. She was aware only of his nearness, his male strength and the warm musky scent of him.

Then, abruptly, Brett withdrew his lips and she was no longer clasped in the steel-strong circle of his arms. She heard his voice as if from far away, chilling her with its bitter scorn.

"You have found more than your match in me, Lynn Forster, so be warned! Keep away from Rafael, or it will be the worse for you." Before she could reply, if indeed she could have summoned the strength to speak at all, he opened the double doors and strode out of the room.

For long, agonised moments Lynn stood where he had left her, feeling shocked and dazed. When at last she left the salon and made her way upstairs, she was thankful that she encountered no other member of the household. Reaching the sanctuary of her bedroom, she did not put on the lights but stood in darkness at the tall window, gazing out at the velvet canopy of the southern night, pricked with a million spangled stars. Slowly, tears formed in her eyes, to run unimpeded down her cheeks, until the stars merged and became blurred drifts of light.

She knew now that she was in love with Brett Sackville. She loved a man who disdained and despised her, who felt even less respect for her than for any of the numerous women he had so casually taken as mistresses. How was it possible, she thought wretchedly, for her to have lost her heart to such a man? Until now, Lynn had believed that she disliked him, even that she hated him. But now, to her bitter humiliation, she had to admit that Brett had awakened in her love and tenderness such as she had never before felt for any man. And never would again. Yet it was a love without happiness, without promise, a love empty of all hope.

# 6

THE short, dark woman named Luzia, whom Lynn by now realised was as much a companion to Señora Alejandro as a personal maid, came to the room which had been equipped as a studio with the request that Lynn should join her mistress for afternoon tea. Slightly apprehensive about the reason for this summons, Lynn went first to her bedroom to change from paint-spattered jeans into a suitable dress.

For the past few days she'd been working hard, having given her opinion that seven of the various landscapes and portraits which graced *Los Pámpanos* were in need of a certain amount of restoration. Her suggestions had been accepted at once, and Rafael had driven her into the nearest town to buy the equipment she needed. Since then, despite Lynn's hints that he must surely have things to do on the estate, Rafael had spent hours pacing restlessly around her studio, trying to persuade her to drop her work and go sightseeing with him, which she steadfastly refused to do.

During this period, Lynn had seen Brett Sackville at the dinner table, and that was all. Much of his time, she gathered, he spent at his firm's office in Cádiz, where Rosa-María's father was manager. One evening Brett did not even appear at dinner, arriving home after Lynn had retired to her room. She wondered if he had been seeing Juanita. There had been no mention of the Spanish woman, from him or anyone else.

Señora Alejandro and her maid-cum-companion occupied a suite of upstairs rooms in the central part of the house. When, ten minutes later, Lynn tapped on the door, it was opened at once by Luzia, who motioned her to enter.

"*La señora* awaits you on the

balcony," she told Lynn, gesturing towards the tall French windows. "Please to go through to her, *señorita*."

The balcony, which offered ample space for several basketwork chairs and a table, was shaded by a canvas awning, and climbing plants made a cool tumbling mass of greenery. Señora Alejandro, reclining comfortably with cushions at her back, greeted Lynn affably.

"Ah, there you are, Miss Forster! I trust I did not disturb you at an inconvenient moment?"

"Not at all, Señora Alejandro," she murmured politely, taking the seat indicated. "I shall enjoy having my tea with you today."

The older woman smiled. "We English! Where would we be without our tea? I have lived in Spain so long that I have become almost Spanish in my ways, yet I still need a cup of tea in the afternoon. Coffee is a delicious beverage in its own way, but it cannot replace tea at this time of day. Don't you agree?"

"Yes, indeed!"

All this, Lynn realised, was no more than a preliminary chat before the real reason her presence was required became apparent. Still feeling apprehensive, she managed to respond to the smalltalk. Did Lynn find the heat of Andalusia enervating? No, she enjoyed it; she always enjoyed the few brief heatwaves in England. Did the nature of her work bring her abroad very much? No, this was the first job she'd ever undertaken away from home, though her father had on occasion accepted commissions on the continent . . . and even in America.

And then came the first question with a recognisable purpose behind it.

"I hope, Miss Forster, that in persuading you to stay here and do this work for us, we are not depriving a young man in England of your company?"

"Not at all," Lynn replied steadily,

"there is no one special in my life at the moment."

"Indeed! You surprise me, my dear . . . such a charming girl as you! Surely you are pursued on all sides by eager young men?"

"Hardly that!" said Lynn, with the faintest of smiles.

"But then," the older woman continued, as if idly, "England is not Spain, eh? Here, the male blood runs hot . . . though, sad to say, ardour so often quickly cools. The young Spaniard is an adept at paying a pretty compliment, bestowing a soulful glance, breathing a heartfelt sigh. He practises these things as a form of artistic expression. But marriage is an altogether more serious matter to him."

She broke off as Luzia emerged from the French doors bearing a tray of tea things . . . an elegant silver teapot and a cream jug of fine bone china delicately patterned with English roses. The maid set the tray down on the table, and Señora Alejandro dismissed her with a smile of thanks.

"I will pour today, Luzia."

She made a little performance of the task, asking Lynn if she preferred cream or lemon, did she take sugar, offering her *petit fours* from an incredibly fragile porcelain basket.

The tea poured, the conversation became purposeful again.

"Miss Forster, I am thinking of arranging a little picnic party tomorrow at our private beach . . . just myself and my two sons, and naturally Rafael's fiancée-to-be! Would you care to join us? I am sure you will find Rosa-María an altogether delightful girl, and of course you will have an escort of your own in Brett. Luzia will be there to look after my needs."

Lynn's hand shook so that her cup rattled in its saucer.

"It's very good of you, Señora Alejandro," she faltered, "but I'm afraid I can't accept. I have so much work to do."

"Oh, but surely . . . you are too diligent, my dear! A little diversion now and then is good for us. Do say that you will come."

While Lynn still hesitated, wondering how she could escape, the other woman added in a pleasant, but firmly decisive voice, "I insist that you join us . . . I positively insist!"

"Well . . . thank you, Señora Alejandro, you are most kind."

"Now, as to plans. We had better assemble at the beach at, say, noon. I shall despatch Rafael in advance to collect Rosa-María — it is a drive of some forty kilometres to Cádiz — while Luzia and I will of course need another car to take us down to the beach, together with the picnic hampers and so on. But, since you say you don't feel the heat unduly, I suggest that you take the opportunity of seeing something of the vineyards by walking there with Brett. I'm sure you will find it interesting. Then another day he will take you to our *bodega* in Sanlúcar de Barrameda.

188

We really cannot permit you to return to England without seeing something of the fascinating processes involved in making sherry."

Lynn was dazed and confused by this blatant attempt to throw her into Brett's company . . . as though his mother's dearest wish was a union between the two of them. It was utterly inexplicable. If Señora Alejandro was so firmly opposed to any romantic attachment between her and Rafael — a fact she had gone to pains to make crystal clear — why was she not concerned about the possibility of the selfsame thing happening with her elder son?

Lynn was back at her easel, staring blindly at the painting propped there, before the answer came to her with a sharp stab of pain. The cunning scheme (for however benign Señora Alejandro might be, it could be called nothing less) had been hatched to pry her and Rafael apart and push him in Rosa-María's direction. And Brett's role, knowingly or unknowingly, was to act as a buffer between her and his brother, to keep them firmly separated. There would be no risk involved, the Señora would argue, for though Rafael might be a vulnerable, impetuous young man, his elder brother was nothing of the kind. Brett's heart was impregnable, a hard, steely thing she would be unable even to dent. Ultimately, when Rafael's straying affections were safely anchored once more to Rosa-María, Lynn could be packed off back to England. And Brett, like everyone else here, would promptly forget all about her.

★ ★ ★

It was yet another day of blazing heat, and Lynn stood waiting for Brett in the shadowed coolness of the hall. He had arrived back from the vineyards only ten minutes ago and gone straight upstairs to shower and change. When he reappeared, he didn't bother to apologise for keeping her hanging around. In response to his surly, "Let's get going, then," she followed him out of doors, blinking in the bright sunlight.

"I understand you want to have a closer look at the vineyards on our way to the beach," he said.

"It was your mother's suggestion," Lynn corrected. "I have no wish to trouble you if it's inconvenient."

"You're hardly dressed for a walk through the vineyards," he observed, indicating her white slacks and cool yellow top. "You'll get smothered in dust."

"Oh, I didn't think of that!" But what did it matter what she looked like . . . she wasn't trying to impress anyone, was she? "Anyway, it's too late to go back and change now," she added defiantly.

He went striding forward so quickly that she had to hurry to keep up with him. When they reached the boundary of the *casa*'s grounds the vineyards began, and Brett took a rough track between orderly rows of vines, which seemed to stretch away into infinity. A sentinel line of umbrella palms followed the course of a dusty roadway and soon they came to a low, white-painted building, its frontage arched in the Spanish style.

"It's a *bodega*," said Brett shortly, in answer to her timid question.

"Oh, I see! I thought a *bodega* was much bigger."

"The word merely means a wine-cellar or warehouse. There's one like this in every vineyard, where the grapes are brought after the harvest in September to be trodden. After the first stage of fermentation, the wine is transported to the large *bodegas* in the towns, where the process of turning it into sherry begins."

"It must be wonderful here at vintage time," she said wistfully.

His dark eyes took on a faraway look and his manner became less imperious.

"Yes, I always try to be in Spain then, if I possibly can. There's an air of festivity over the whole country-side that is infectious. The women sing in the fields as they gather the grape harvest, and the *pisadores* — that's the men who tread the grapes in huge wooden troughs — have a traditional song of their own. Suddenly all the roads seem full of curious two-wheeled carts drawn by oxen, carrying the great butts of new wine, and the aroma of fermentation is all around in the air."

Carried away by his enthusiasm, Lynn exclaimed without thinking, "It sounds marvellous! I wish I could be here then."

This time her words had quite a different effect on him. He replied in a steel-hard voice, "No doubt you would, Miss Forster, but you will have long returned to England by that time. Make no mistake about it!"

She coloured violently before his censorious gaze. "I fully realise that! I . . . I just meant that it sounds exciting, the way you described it."

They walked on in silence for a while,

until they reached a place where the land took on a craggy formation, the vines cultivated here in small, terraced fields. At a high vantage point they suddenly came in sight of the ocean, a shimmering expanse of liquid gold. Brett came to an abrupt halt and Lynn stopped too, to admire the view. The beauty of it somehow made her acutely conscious of the man beside her, of his nearness. If only, she thought wistfully, the relationship between them could have been the normal happy one between a man and a woman enjoying a walk in these exotic surroundings. But between her and Brett Sackville there was only joyless, unwanted love on her side, and distrust and brooding hostility on his.

The extent of his hostility was made immediately apparent when he said in an abrupt tone, "I suggest, Miss Forster, that you accept with as much grace as possible that your presence at *La Casa de los Pámpanos* is ill-judged and regrettable in the extreme.

Nevertheless, you will be extended every courtesy while you are here, *provided* you concentrate on your work. But try playing any tricks, and it will be the worse for you. I am determined that you shan't be allowed to ruin the relationship between my brother and Rosa-María."

"Does your trusteeship over Rafael entitle you to make the choice of a wife for him, too?" she asked with bitter sarcasm.

Staring out to sea, Lynn didn't observe the effect of her words, but she heard Brett catch his breath in annoyance.

"If you had a younger brother," he said, barely controlling his patience, "would you be willing to stand by and watch him ruin his entire future for the sake of what amounts to an adolescent infatuation?"

"Rafael is not an adolescent," Lynn pointed out. "He is twenty-three. Perfectly competent, I would have thought, to make his own decisions."

"I am aware that you are only twenty-three yourself — a few months younger than my brother, in fact. Yet while you're already a fully mature woman he is still very youthful, and needs to be kept from making a fool of himself. We both know that for a fact, Miss Forster, so it is pointless for you to pretend otherwise."

She hated him for always driving her into a corner ... hated him, and yet loved him! Even as she felt white-hot anger, a need to strike out and hurt him as he was hurting her, she felt an equal yearning to be held once again in his arms, to feel once again his lips bruising hers in a hard, passionate kiss.

"Rafael means nothing to me ... not in the way you mean," she said in a low, dispirited voice. "I have told *him* that, and I have told you. How many times must I repeat it to be believed?"

"If Rafael still pursues you with hope in his heart, it can only be because your protestations are unconvincing. In other words, your coy denials are calculated to increase his interest in you, not to diminish it."

Lynn felt almost desperate. "Then please tell me how I can convince you — and Rafael — that I really mean what I say. Just tell me!" she begged.

In her misery, she unintentionally put a hand on his arm, and Brett shook her off as though she had stung him.

"We had better go," he said icily. "The others will have arrived long ago, and they'll be wondering what has become of us."

★ ★ ★

The Alejandros' private beach was a crescent of pale golden sand, hemmed in by rugged rocky outcrops. Where the tracks came to an end, a chalet gleamed whitely in the sun, a miniature Moorish palace of slender minarets and fretted archways showing the shadowed coolness within. Nearby two cars were parked — Rafael's, and the one which had brought Señora Alejandro and her maid Luzia. Chairs and a couple of tables had been set up in the shade of a huge green canvas awning, and the manservant who had chauffeured the two older women was offering drinks on a tray. A picnic, Lynn noted wryly, was hardly an apt description for this elegant occasion!

Her eyes went at once to the only member of the party she had not so far met. Rosa-María was petite and lovely, with raven-black hair and huge dark eyes which looked out at the world with a kind of veiled timidity. The girl's demeanour reminded Lynn once again that Spain had for many centuries been overrun by the Moors, who had kept their womenfolk hidden in the traditional *purdah*.

Introductions were made, and Lynn and Brett took the chairs awaiting them. Sipping a cool drink, Lynn tried to avoid the jealously reproachful look in Rafael's eyes.

"It is foolish to walk so far in the sun like that," he muttered. And glancing round to make sure that his mother couldn't overhear, he added, "One of those eccentric English habits — like arranging a picnic in the heat of the day!"

Lynn gave him a faint, nervous smile.

"We get so little sunshine like this in England that I suppose it's only natural that we enjoy it so much."

"You like *España* much better than England, *sí*?" he demanded eagerly.

"No . . . I didn't say that," she replied cautiously, aware that Brett was watching her with critical eyes.

There were changing rooms in the chalet, and the four younger members of the party went inside to don their beachwear; Lynn's and Brett's had been brought in the car for them. Lynn had been careful to equip herself with a new swimsuit before leaving England, something in place of her revealing yellow bikini. This one was navy and white, an altogether more demure, one-piece garment, but slick and well-cut so that it did full justice to her trim figure. When she put it on, Rosa-María gave an envious sigh.

"I am jealous of your lovely English complexion," she confessed shyly. "And your long legs and slim hips give you such elegance. I wish I was not so short and . . . how do you say — dumpy?"

"But you're not!" Lynn protested sincerely. "And that black swimsuit sets off the beautiful warm tones of your skin. Honestly, you've no reason to be jealous of me, Rosa-María."

"Have I not?" The soft, elusive eyes met Lynn's for a fleeting instant, then slid away. "I think that men find tall English girls very attractive, no?"

Lynn smiled awkwardly. "I'm sure you must be greatly admired by the opposite sex."

"But that I do not wish!"

"Oh, come now! Doesn't every woman want male admiration?"

"For me, from one man only," the

girl replied simply, adding, "Perhaps it is different here than in England?"

"No, I don't suppose it's very different anywhere in the world. However much she might like men in general to admire her, a girl always has one special man she wants to fall in love with her." Even as the words left her lips, Lynn was consumed by a feeling of bleak despair. For her there was indeed one special man, the only man who mattered a jot to her. And she had seen the contempt and scorn in Brett's eyes, in his whole demeanour, when he looked at her. "It doesn't always work out, though," she added desolately, hardly aware that she had said the words aloud. "Sometimes we choose a man who will *never* love us."

They were both changed and ready to join the men, but still Rosa-María hung back.

"You met Rafael in England, I believe?" she probed.

"Yes. He called at his brother's house in England, where I was working on some paintings."

"Rafael is saying how very clever you are. He . . . he speaks of little else." Her solemn young eyes clouded with hurt. "He is changed, since he came back."

"I expect it's only temporary," said Lynn uncomfortably. "Men do get moody sometimes, but I'm sure Rafael will soon get over it." She forced a smile. "Come on, we'd better go outside, or they'll wonder what's become of us."

The two men were talking to their mother. Seeing them together in swim trunks, the difference between them was somehow accentuated. Rafael's skin gleamed smooth and olive-tinted in the sunshine, and his build was noticeably stockier than his half-brother's. Brett's well-knit frame, even when totally relaxed in repose, seemed to possess the quality of a coiled steel spring, ready to leap into dynamic action at any moment. He wore briefly-cut, pale-blue trunks, and the gold band of his watch still circled his wrist, echoing the gleam of gold from the slim chain around his neck.

Seeing the girls emerge the two men stood up, and Rafael suggested, "Let's go for a swim before lunch."

Brett nodded, his dark eyes giving Lynn such a leisurely appraisal that she knew he was deliberately reminding her of the occasions in England when much more of her body had been revealed to him.

"You'd better stick close by me, Miss Forster. The current here is a little tricky for someone who doesn't know it." Pausing, Brett added in a voice meant to be overheard by all, "Isn't it high time I started calling you Lynn, by the way? And you must call me Brett."

In other circumstances Lynn would have been thrilled to have him drop the formalities, but she knew Brett was only doing it for the effect it would have on his brother. And, indeed, Rafael's expression hardened in disapproval, even though he himself had used Lynn's first name from the very beginning.

In the water, Brett always contrived to be between her and Rafael. Once, when a small wave went over her head, catching her by surprise and making her gulp for air, his hands shot out quickly to support her. His touch was brief, yet when he let her go again, her body throbbed with the remembered pressure of his fingers.

Ten minutes later, when the foursome left the water and walked up the beach, Lynn felt Brett's gaze upon her and was embarrassingly aware that her swimsuit clung wetly to her figure. Somehow Brett always had this ability to make her feel naked under his relentless, probing scrutiny. She longed to change back into her clothes, but none of the others showed any signs of wanting to, and Lynn felt she couldn't make a point of doing so herself.

After they'd eaten . . . a delicious meal which commenced with an ice-cold soup made from tomatoes and cucumbers, followed by a multitude of cold meats and crisp salads . . . and naturally some cool, clear wine from the Alejandro vineyards, Lynn wandered off to gather some of the pretty shells scattered across the beach. Glancing back, she decided that no one was watching her so she slipped out of sight among the rocks, wanting to be alone with her unhappy thoughts.

The rocks here, washed by the Atlantic tides, were studded with little pools in which small fish darted to and fro and baby crabs lingered, trapped until the next high tide. Presently, Lynn knelt and stared down into one of the pools, fascinated by this close-up view of marine life. She could see her own reflection staring back at her, outlined against the bright blue of the sky.

The ceaseless swish of waves breaking on the shore must have obliterated the sound of someone approaching. The first Lynn knew was the reflection of a face beside hers, a face so superficially like that of the man she loved that

Lynn mistook it for him and spun round quickly, her pulses leaping.

But the man standing over her was Rafael, not Brett, and she tried to cover her instinctive disappointment by saying a cheerful "Hello!"

Rafael was smiling down at her. "We're alone at last, thank heaven! Oh, but what a stupid business this picnic is! I do not know what possessed *Madre* to arrange it."

"Yes you do!" said Lynn steadily. "Your mother is making sure you spend plenty of time in Rosa-María's company. She thinks you are neglecting the poor girl . . . and it's true, you are."

Rafael curled his lips in a childish pout.

"I am bored with Rosa-María, she seems so young and . . . and immature. It is you I love, Lynn — you know that."

Lynn remained crouched by the pool, feeling that in some way it helped to keep a little distance between them.

"You are being very unkind, Rafael! Rosa-María adores you; you know she does. The light of love is in her eyes, quite unmistakably, every time she looks at you."

"And do you not see the light of love in *my* eyes, *cara*, when I look at *you*?"

Sighing, Lynn started to rise to her feet with the intention of telling Rafael in no uncertain terms that she really meant what she'd told him so many times before . . . that she did not, could not, and never would love him. That she was convinced the love he professed to feel for her was no more than a youthful infatuation. But as she stood upright her foot slipped on the weed covered rock and she toppled. Her arms flailed wildly as she tried to regain her balance, then suddenly she was caught and held safe. Rafael's arms were around her, and his face was only millimeters from hers.

"Oh, *querida*!" he breathed. "I want

always to hold you close like this, and never to let you go."

Lynn struggled unavailingly against him. "No . . . no, Rafael, you mustn't! Let me go!"

But his grip on her only tightened and she could feel the pounding of his heart, pressed close against her. The next instant his mouth had come down on hers in a passionate kiss.

"Rafael!"

Brett's voice, coming from behind her, was like a whiplash. She felt Rafael's start of surprise, and he released her from his arms, looking sheepish.

"What is it now, Brett?" he muttered sullenly.

"Mother wants you," his brother replied. "Please go to her at once."

Rafael hesitated for one mutinous moment, then gave a shrug of acquiescence. Holding out his hand to Lynn, he said, "Here, let me help you over these rocks or you might trip a second time. If I had not caught you just now, you'd have fallen into that pool."

"No, go at once, Rafael," Brett commanded. "I will see Lynn safely back across the rocks."

"Oh, very well!"

Rafael walked off disconsolately and Lynn made to follow him. But Brett shot out an arm to prevent her.

"Just a minute, I've something to say to you!"

"Look, if you're thinking I wanted Rafael to kiss me just then," she began, "you're quite mistaken. I slipped on the rock and he saved me from falling. The . . . the kiss was a sudden impulse on his part."

"I've no doubt it was . . . on *his* part! But not on yours. Doubtless you had it all neatly planned so as to end up in his arms, looking provocative and appealing."

Lynn stared back at him in misery. It was beyond bearing, the strange combination of love and loathing she felt for this man. Right now, she had an almost uncontrollable urge to throw herself into his arms. But those strong arms of his would not close lovingly around her body as she so fiercely desired. She would meet only cold rejection from him . . . or be subjected to another of those kisses of sheer contempt, designed to show her that she was just as capable as he was of passion without any sense of committment, of selfishly seeking physical gratification with none of the tenderness that went with real love.

With a scarcely audible sigh, Lynn turned away from him and began scrambling across the rocks, not knowing where she was going or whether she could hope to escape from his hectoring voice. Perhaps it was inevitable that in trying to hurry over such rough terrain she should come to grief. A rock that appeared solid and safe tipped under the weight of Lynn's foot and she was flung headlong, falling heavily on her elbow. And from her ankle came a searing stab of pain.

Brett was there in an instant, crouching down beside her.

"What is it? Are you hurt?" he demanded.

"It . . . it's my left ankle," she gasped, wincing in agony.

Brett knelt and felt the injured ankle with gently probing fingers. "I think it's virtually certain there's nothing broken, but we mustn't take any chances."

With that, he lifted her bodily into his arms and began to carry her, heading back across the rocky shore. He seemed to bear her weight with no effort, but it was difficult for him to keep his balance on the uneven ground, so he ordered Lynn to put an arm around his neck.

Somehow it was unbearably poignant to be clinging to him so intimately, feeling his naked chest separated from her own flesh merely by the thin fabric of her swimsuit. She could feel his shoulder muscles rippling beneath her hand, and his breath was warm against her cheek. A tiny involuntary shiver ran through her and at once Lynn felt a sense of panic.

Considering attack to be the best form of defense, she cried, "I suppose you think my fall was all neatly planned this time, too?"

"I've considered the question and decided not," he replied calmly. "You'd have risked doing yourself a serious injury, and to no purpose, because my young brother would soon lose interest in you if you were laid up for any length of time. No, this has been a happy accident for you. A slightly sprained ankle will no doubt bestow you with an added romantic aura . . . a fact you will doubtless make full use of."

"Oh, you're impossible!" she burst out wretchedly. "Must you always be so cynical and put the very worst interpretation on every single thing I do?"

She tried to lever herself away from him, too burningly aware of his closeness. But he held her more tightly so she could scarcely move.

"Keep still," he rapped, "or you'll have us both over." His voice carried a dangerous note and Lynn instantly obeyed. But she muttered sullenly,

"You don't have to carry me, you know. I could manage by myself."

"Yes, you'd enjoy that . . . letting the others see how brave you were, hobbling painfully across the beach so that my brother would come rushing forward to help you, full of solicitude. At least I can prevent that."

This time Lynn didn't answer him. She couldn't have done so, because her throat was suddenly thick with tears. A tiny sob escaped her, and Brett paused and turned his head to look at her.

"I'm sorry if I was a bit rough on you," he muttered apologetically. "I do realise you're really hurt. That ankle *is* very swollen and it must be pretty painful."

The unexpected concern in his voice proved too much for Lynn. Her tears really began to flow, and she closed her eyes and kept her face averted to try and hide them from him. Brett didn't move on again, and she could sense that he was still looking at her. Then, from out of nowhere, she felt a feather-light touch upon her hair. Had Brett kissed her . . . a gentle kiss of tenderness and compassion? Or was it just a creation of her imagination, born of a vibrant inner longing?

Lynn kept her eyes closed, scared of discovering that she had been mistaken, and that his gaze held only the scorn and contempt she had come to dread. She would steadfastly believe that he had kissed her, against all probability, against all reason. Unconsciously, she snuggled even closer to him, her softness yielding to the hardness of his body.

A car was coming down the track to the beach, its engine revving angrily. But Lynn was barely conscious of it and neither, for all the reaction he showed, was Brett. Then suddenly, as they emerged from behind the rocks onto the open beach, a voice charged with outrage caused him to stop in his tracks.

"So, Brett, I go to Madrid for a few days, and return to find this! What is the explanation of such behaviour?"

Startled, Lynn turned her head to see Juanita coming towards them, her eyes blazing.

"I wish an explanation, Brett," the Spanish woman repeated dangerously, a complete virago.

"For heaven's sake, Juanita," Brett replied impatiently, walking on again, "can't you see that Lynn is hurt?"

"*Madre de Dios!* What has happened?" It was Rafael, who came rushing up to them in alarm. "Oh, what has she done? My poor Lynn, this is dreadful!"

"Get out of the way, Rafael," Brett ordered impatiently. "She's given her ankle a nasty twist. Prepare a compress someone . . . a towel wrung out in water as cold as possible. Use some ice."

He laid her down gently on a long basket chair that had a footrest, cradling her injured ankle with soft cushions. It was Rosa-María who, with quiet and unfussy efficiency, produced the cold compress. Between them, she and Brett bandaged Lynn's ankle, the girl's fingers quick and dextrous, the man's caring and infinitely gentle.

Juanita stood over them, watching with jealous eyes. But in contrast, Rosa-María's distrust of Lynn was gone, wiped away by seeing her borne so tenderly in Brett's arms. Lynn herself, looking up at him as he bent over her, found it difficult to believe now that only moments ago her cheek had nestled against the warm contours of his sunburnt chest, where the dark hairs curled with springy softness.

"All this ridiculous fussing about a twisted ankle!" Juanita grumbled. "It is nothing . . . nothing at all." She gestured peremptorily at the manservant, who was also looking on. "If everyone is so concerned, then Julio had better drive her back to the house and let her rest in her bedroom. That is the best place for her."

Señora Alejandro, giving Juanita a rebukeful glance, took charge of the arrangements and announced in a firm, decisive tone,

"We will all of us go now, I think . . . it is almost too hot for comfort. Rosa-María, will you come back to the house for a while before Rafael drives you home? And Brett . . . put Miss Forster in the back seat of the car; use some cushions to protect her ankle. Luzia and I will travel in the front beside Julio." Lastly, she fixed her gaze upon Juanita again, and there was no liking or warmth in her eyes. "I'm sorry we are leaving when you have only just arrived, Juanita, but you are welcome, of course, to use the beach for as long as you like. Please give my regards to your father when you return home."

Juanita shrugged, scarcely even bothering to glance at the older woman. Her black, flashing eyes riveted on Lynn, sending an unmistakable message. "You may have won this round," she was saying viciously, "but the final triumph will be mine . . . make no mistake about that!"

# 7

ROSA-MARÍA spent many hours
sitting chatting with Lynn, who
found her presence soothing.
The suggestion that the young Spanish
girl should not return home to Cádiz,
but instead stay on a few days at *Los
Pámpanos*, had come as an inspiration
to Señora Alejandro.

"You and Miss Forster will be nice
company for each other while she has
this wretchedly painful ankle," she'd
said enthusiastically. "And it will give
you and Rafael the opportunity to see
more of each other than if you were
forty kilometres apart."

Artless pleasure had shone in Rosa-
María's velvet-soft eyes.

"Oh, *muchas gracias*, Doña Victoria
— I shall be so happy to stay."

At Brett's insistence, a doctor had
been called in to see Lynn. He had

gravely examined her injured ankle, prodded and pressed it, and finally pronounced that no damage had been done beyond a simple sprain. Resting up for a day or two was all the treatment necessary, he added. Since Lynn needed to be on her feet to do her work, she'd been forced to abandon the easel for a while. She and Rosa-María had been closeted together in a small morning room which afforded a charming view of the grounds, the wide French windows thrown open to the flower-scented air.

Lynn was idly leafing through an illustrated Spanish fashion magazine, trying to understand some of the captions, when Rosa-María said suddenly, "I think you like Brett, no? I think you like him very much."

Startled, Lynn took a tight grip on herself before answering. She endeavored to sound casual, indifferent.

"Oh, I wouldn't say that. I mean, he's very pleasant, of course, and naturally I don't *dislike* him. But beyond that . . . well, I think you've got the wrong idea, Rosa-María."

"I think I have not!" the younger girl contradicted with a tiny, secret smile. "I have observed, Lynn, the way you look at him."

Lynn flushed, then felt a sharp prick of anger at betraying herself, which only made the flush deepen. Realising that it was useless to refute Rosa-María's assertion, she tried to minimise her feelings.

"Well, you must admit that he's a very attractive man," she said lightly, giving a little gurgle of laughter. "I don't think any girl would be completely immune to him. Unless, like you," she added cunningly, "she has already found the right man for her."

"Ah, yes . . . !" Rosa-María's eyes became dreamy, but after a moment she returned to her theme. "And Brett finds you attractive, Lynn, so all is well."

"Oh, no," Lynn denied swiftly, "you're quite wrong there!"

Rosa-María shook her head stubbornly. "I do not imagine that which I see in Brett's eyes. Already he is beginning to fall in love with you. I am so pleased for you, Lynn, I cannot express."

Lynn sought for a suitable answer to this. How could she tell Rosa-María the plain, unpalatable truth . . . that Brett was deliberately giving the false impression of being attracted to her simply to discourage Rafael from harbouring romantic dreams about her? It would be too cruel, when Rosa-María was just beginning to feel renewed confidence in her power to hold Rafael's love. Besides which, a tiny voice within her was insisting against all reason, perhaps it wasn't *entirely* make-believe on Brett's part. The memory of that feather-light kiss upon her hair when he was carrying her back across the beach refused to be dismissed.

"Brett isn't the type to fall in love," she said at last, adopting a tone of brittle worldliness. "Okay, so he sees me as a reasonably attractive girl. That's why he might have spared me a second glance, Rosa-María. But you can be sure that if he has any ideas about me — which I doubt — they aren't *romantic* ideas. Any involvement he envisages with a woman would leave him free and unfettered — Brett's very own words, mark you — and unscathed!"

The young girl's eyes clouded with distress. "Alas, I know this to be true about men. Even my own Rafael. I realise that before we fell in love, he . . . well, there were women. It is something we just have to accept as a part of their nature, I think. Men are not angels!" Then she brightened, and her lovely oval face became a picture of youthful eagerness. "But however free in their behaviour they have been before, Lynn, they change when they meet the right girl. Love alters everything, you will see."

Feeling a lump in her throat, Lynn smiled at the young, innocent girl. "I'm glad you are so happy with Rafael. The two of you make a lovely couple, Rosa-María."

She blushed. "Rafael is so handsome, do you not agree? So noble! I want more than anything in the world to become his wife. I . . . I think it will not be long now before he asks me." She hesitated fleetingly, then plunged on with a confession, as though she felt impelled to make it. "Lynn . . . when Rafael did not come to see me right away on his return to *España*, and . . . and I heard he had brought back a girl from England with him, I was afraid . . . well, I began to feel very jealous of you."

"You have no need for jealousy," Lynn assured her in a low voice. "No need at all."

"*Sí*, I know that now. When Rafael came to fetch me for the picnic, and then . . . when you and Brett arrived together on the beach and I saw how he looked at you, how tenderly he carried you in his arms when you were hurt, I had no fears left."

Absently, Lynn plucked at a button on her dress, till she realised she was making it loose.

"Juanita is a very beautiful woman, don't you think?" she said in a casual voice. "It's no wonder that men find her irresistible."

Rosa-María made a face of disapproval. "I do not like Juanita. She . . . she flaunts herself at men in the most shameful way."

"Tell me about her," Lynn requested. "I know she's a widow, of course, and that her father owns a big horse farm near here. But that's about all."

"Juanita's father is a very wealthy man, and he indulges her in every possible way. Her husband too, who died about two years ago . . . he allowed Juanita great freedom, which is not our way here in *España*."

"Who was her husband?" Lynn asked curiously.

"Gregorio Vazquez, a well-known film director. He travelled a great deal when working on location, and sometimes Juanita went with him. But more often she stayed at home and enjoyed herself. Always, even when he was alive, she had intrigues with other men."

"How long has Brett known her?" asked Lynn probingly.

Frowning, Rosa-María put a hand on Lynn's arm in a comforting gesture.

"You must not worry about her, Lynn . . . you must not even think about her and Brett. Whatever there has been between them, I am positive it is all over now."

"Would Juanita agree with you, I wonder?"

Rosa-María shrugged dismissively. "She is a woman who never gives up gracefully. Perhaps she sees in Brett a fine new husband whom she could twist around her finger, but I think not."

"No, she could never do that with Brett," agreed Lynn with utter conviction, and the thought brought a tiny glow of consolation.

After tea that day, Lynn felt recovered enough to try a spell at her easel again. She was at present working on a portrait of the founder of the Alejandro vineyards, a handsome, middle-aged man dressed in the costume of an eighteenth century Spanish grandee. The painting had aged very badly; the layers of old varnish had spread a layer of dingy brown over the entire surface. Lynn worked methodically, and when she packed up for the day she had cleared another few square inches, exposing the bright glowing colours of the paint underneath.

She stood back for a few minutes studying it in satisfaction. To her professional eye, the painting was coming along nicely, but at this early stage it inevitably looked rather patchy. It struck Lynn that since this particular portrait was of considerable sentimental value to the family it might be as well that no one saw her work until it was more advanced. So, shaking out a square of white cloth from her box of equipment, she carefully draped it over the easel. With a last check to see that everything was in order, she left the room and went upstairs to change for dinner, limping a little on her injured ankle.

Juanita came to dinner that evening, uninvited. It was evident from a certain tightness of the lips that Señora Alejandro was not pleased, though courtesy to a friend of the family forbade any more definite show of displeasure. Over the meal, the conversation turned on Lynn's work, and she explained precisely what she was doing at the moment.

Señora Alejandro said excitedly, "Don Fernando was such a handsome man from all accounts, and I've always thought his portrait didn't do him justice. It will be wonderful to have him looking just as he did when the portrait was painted nearly two hundred years ago."

"No painting can ever be restored completely to its original condition,"

Lynn hastened to point out. "That's just not possible. But I can certainly make the portrait look a great deal better than it has done for a long time now."

Juanita, the spite in her eyes visible only to Lynn, remarked as though interestedly, "Yes, I have seen what you do have I not, Señorita Forster? You use a bottle of cleaning fluid and rub it over the picture with cotton wool until the colours are bright."

"I'm sure there is far more still required than you suggest, Juanita," her hostess reprimanded. Then, as if wanting to make a point of her faith in Lynn's expertise, she added, "Perhaps I might be permitted to see you at work, Miss Forster. I am sure it is a fascinating process to watch. I will look in on you tomorrow morning."

This was exactly what Lynn was anxious to avoid at this stage. "I . . . I'm afraid there won't be much for you to see, *señora*, because I have only just started on this painting. Perhaps you could leave it for two or three days?"

"But of course, if that is what you suggest."

Grateful for the respite, Lynn caught Brett's gaze across the table. He was regarding her speculatively, a question lurking in his dark eyes. But he made no comment.

Immediately after they took coffee in the lamplit salon, Señora Alejandro withdrew to her private suite. Brett too disappeared, saying something about having some work to finish, and when soon afterwards Juanita also left the room, Lynn guessed that she had gone to join him by prearrangement. An agonising picture formed in her mind of the two of them coming together, flinging themselves into each other's arms in a passionate embrace. It was quite true, Lynn felt convinced, that Brett would never allow himself to be trapped into marriage by Juanita, but it seemed little consolation right now to know that he was only using the Spanish girl for his own selfish gratification. For a fleeting instant Lynn wished with a burning intensity that she could be in Juanita's place at this very moment, that *she* was locked in Brett's strong arms in some shadowed room, or wandering hand-in-hand through the moonlit grounds, pausing often to kiss and murmur the low-voiced endearments that lovers exchange . . .

"Poor Lynn, you look so forlorn sitting there. Is your ankle still painful?"

It was Rafael, who had deserted Rosa-María and come across to where she sat upon a brocade sofa, pretending to be absorbed in a book.

"Not really! It's so much better now that I hardly notice it."

Lynn glanced covertly at Rosa-María and saw that she was watching them, though as yet showing no great anxiety. Determined not to allow Rafael to give the girl any cause for renewed jealousy, Lynn smiled at her and called, "Why not come over here, and let us play cards. You can teach me one of your

Spanish games."

Rafael brought cards, and they sat down to play. And when, a little later, Juanita returned to the salon, alone, she came and glanced over Lynn's shoulder sneeringly. None of them wanted her company, that was evident, but Rafael invited reluctantly, "Why don't you join in?"

"*Muchas gracias*, but I do not wish to play children's games," she said scornfully. "I have better things to do with my time. Does anyone know where Brett has gone?"

It was clearly an attempt to pretend that they had not been together until just now, Lynn thought miserably, and a very inept one! Why did Juanita trouble to dissemble, unless perhaps Brett had told her to?

"Brett said he had some work to do," Rafael replied, adding with a resigned shrug, "Always, he is working at something or other. Never will that brother of mine relax and enjoy himself."

Juanita flicked a smile of pure malice at Lynn.

"Oh, you are so wrong, my dear Rafael," she cried with a ripple of laughter. "Given the right company, Brett knows better than most men how to enjoy . . . the pleasures of life."

"As doubtless you know from personal experience?" Rafael observed with a meaningful grin.

Juanita's pencil-thin black eyebrows arched superciliously.

"I have never pretended that Brett and I are not . . . close," she drawled. "He is my sort of person, and I am his. It is not surprising that we get on so well together."

Rosa-María, greatly daring, emerged from her shell of shyness to say in a breathless little rush, "I wonder if Brett would agree with that."

"You wonder if I would agree with what, Rosa-María?" demanded a clipped voice from the doorway behind them.

A scarlet flush suffused the young

girl's face, and even Juanita looked abashed. Rafael was undaunted, however, and seized the opportunity to bait his older brother.

"We were talking about you and Juanita, Brett . . . speculating about the exact nature of your relationship."

"This is entirely untrue, Rafael, and you know it," cried Juanita furiously. "Do not believe him, Brett, he is merely trying to make trouble."

Brett looked at them one by one, his face devoid of expression. Lynn's turn came last, and his dark eyes lingered upon her.

"I want to talk to you, Lynn," he said sharply. "Will you come with me, please."

Lynn was no longer conscious of the others as she met his unyielding gaze and tried to read his mind. His face still gave no clue to his mood. Was he angry with her?

She followed Brett out into the hall, and was astonished when he led the way to her 'studio.' Throwing open the door, he flicked on the lights.

"Perhaps you will kindly explain this," he said coldly, gesturing towards the painting on the easel, from which she noticed that someone had removed the white cover.

"I . . . I don't understand," she faltered. "What's the matter?"

"Why pretend?" he asked bitterly. "I want to know how it is that you — supposedly an expert art restorer — could be so criminally careless with a picture entrusted to your care."

Bewildered, Lynn ran forward to look more closely, and gave a horrified gasp. Across the face of Don Fernando was a large patch of smeared paint which obliterated one eye and half the nose. It was apparent to her in that first second that someone had vigorously rubbed the surface of the painting with some of the varnish solvent she used.

"Well?" Brett demanded ominously. "I'm waiting for your explanation."

Lynn regarded him helplessly, icy fingers clawed down her spine.

"I . . . I can't give you an explanation," she stammered. "I can only suppose that this was done deliberately, out of malice."

His expression showed deep disgust. "Do you have to keep up this stupid pretence? It is perfectly obvious to me what happened. This damage was caused by your clumsiness . . . or your lack of expertise! And now you want to dodge the blame."

"But that's absolutely crazy!" Her indignation at this monstrous charge overrode her discretion. "If I had done any damage — which I certainly did not — it would be confined to a tiny patch. You have seen for yourself that I work with just the tip of a little cotton swab. How do you suppose that I could cause damage like this over such a big area?"

His steel-hard eyes did not waver as he stared at her accusingly.

"You can't wriggle out of this so easily," he said, in a voice so chilling that it made her think his blazing

236

anger would be preferable. "There's too much else to be explained away."

"How do you mean?" she asked, mystified.

"For instance, why did you so carefully cover your easel with a sheet? And another thing, why else were you so anxious that my mother shouldn't come and watch you at work for several days, if it wasn't to give yourself a chance to repair the damage?"

"The reason I covered Don Fernando's portrait is simply that I didn't want anyone to see it in its present state . . ."

"That's exactly what I'm saying."

"But not for the reason you think," she insisted. "You've seen my way of working . . . on one small area at a time. So when a painting is half done it looks like a lot of haphazard patches with no method behind them. To an untrained eye, it would look a real mess. That was the only reason I didn't want anyone to see it at this stage."

"You've never covered up any of

the paintings you've been working on before," he accused.

"That's true. But I know that this portrait means a great deal to your mother, so I was extra cautious. It certainly wasn't to conceal that damage from her or from anyone else — because the painting wasn't damaged when I finished work this evening."

"Still trying to wriggle out of blame?" he sneered. "I prefer people who are ready to own up to their mistakes and face the consequences. Who do you suggest was responsible, if it wasn't you?" he added sarcastically. "One of the servants?"

"I . . . I don't know," she faltered miserably. Then on a sudden thought, she asked, "Just now, after dinner . . . was Juanita with you the whole time?"

His eyes flickered, then his expression became thunderous.

"If you're making an accusation against Juanita, you'd better come straight out with it. I don't like innuendoes."

Now that the idea had come to Lynn, it went searing through her brain. Of course, it was the obvious explanation! Juanita would delight in doing anything to bring discredit upon her . . . perhaps cause her to be packed off back to England ignominiously. Hadn't Lynn seen the Spanish woman's jealous eyes, and listened to her spiteful jibes? A memory flashed before her . . . Juanita, at The Spanish House back in England, grabbing up a ball of cotton wool and scrubbing wildly at the horse painting of Brett's that Lynn was working on. Horrified, Lynn had told her then of the damage that could so easily be caused to delicate, aging paint. So Juanita must have remembered — and put her knowledge to vicious use.

Lynn looked up and forced herself to meet Brett's implacable gaze.

"You haven't answered my question yet," she said.

His dark eyes sparked with anger.

"No, and I damned well don't intend to! It's none of your business where I was, or where Juanita was. Now, about this painting . . . can you put the damage right, or is it beyond your skill?"

"I . . . I think I can!" she stammered wretchedly. "If I can find some sort of reference to guide me. Another picture of the same man, perhaps."

He nodded brusquely. "There are two others in the house. I'll have a servant bring them to you in the morning. For my mother's sake, Miss Forster, I am prepared to overlook your ineptitude. But don't expect me to forget your cheap attempt at deceit. That is something I shall never forgive you for."

As the door slammed behind Brett's departing figure, the sound seemed to echo and re-echo round the room. Lynn stood at her easel, trembling violently, her heart crying out against the injustice of it all.

Despairingly, she looked for some

telltale evidence of Juanita's act of sabotage . . . for she hadn't the smallest particle of doubt that the Spanish woman was responsible. But of course, Juanita had been careful to cover her traces. The bottle of solvent was properly stoppered, and whatever rag or ball of cotton wool she had used to apply the liquid was nowhere to be seen, so she must have taken it with her for disposal.

At length, her eyes hazy with tears, Lynn turned and left the room, making her way across the great arched hallway to the marble staircase. With her foot on the first tread, she heard her name called. Rafael was just emerging from the salon with Rosa-María.

"What is it Lynn?" he asked, his voice full of concern for her, and the girl added perceptively, "Have you quarrelled with Brett? You look upset."

Lynn's throat was too choked for speech. Giving a helpless little gesture, she continued on up the stairs as quickly as she could on her still shaky legs, conscious of them staring after her in astonishment.

Safe inside her room, Lynn sank down upon the bed. She felt bruised and beaten, almost as if Brett had struck her with vicious physical blows instead of merely verbal ones. One part of her yearned to escape from Spain . . . from Brett. But she could not escape. Not only because he had insisted that she stay to carry out the work she was commissioned to do. Not only because she was now honour-bound to remain long enough to rectify the malicious damage to the portrait. But most of all because another, stronger, part of her refused to leave. Despite the scorn and abuse he had heaped upon her, she still couldn't voluntarily tear herself away from the man who had captured her heart.

The big house seemed silent as the grave. Once, lost in her misery, Lynn was startled into sudden awareness by the sound of a departing car. It must, she decided dully, be Juanita leaving.

Was Brett going with her to see her home, or had he already bidden her a lover's goodnight?

At long last, she rose from the bed and somehow found the energy to undress and prepare herself for the night. The water soothed her fevered skin, and the soft night air was wonderfully cool when she separated the curtain and stepped out for a few moments onto the jasmine-scented balcony, standing in the darkness in nothing but her thin shortie nightdress. Then, slipping back into the room, she was in the act of crossing to the bed when she was startled by a quiet tapping on the door.

"Who is it?" she called wonderingly.

There was no reply, only a more urgent tapping. Lynn hesitated, then drawing on her short dressing-gown and hastily knotting the sash around her waist, she went to open the door.

"Rafael!" she gasped in surprise. "What do you want?"

Putting a warning finger to his lips,

he quickly stepped inside and silently closed the door behind him.

"Lynn, I had to come," he began. "Brett has been a brute to you, has he not? I sensed something when he came to the salon for you . . . and then later, when Rosa-María and I saw you on the staircase, it was obvious you were deeply upset. I could say nothing then, of course. But ever since, I have been longing to come and comfort you. Only now, when the house is quiet, did I consider it prudent."

"You shouldn't have come at all, Rafael," she chided him. "It's very sweet of you to worry about me, but there's no need."

"How can I help myself, Lynn . . . feeling as I do about you?" He came and put his hands on her shoulders, gazing deeply into her eyes. "Tell me what Brett said to you. Then I shall have it out with him. He cannot be allowed to . . . to insult you and get away with it."

"No, you mustn't say anything to

him," cried Lynn in alarm. If Brett were to discover that she and Rafael had been exchanging confidences — and in her room late at night! — things would be ten times worse than they were now.

"I shall decide that for myself," said Rafael solemnly. "I am a man of honour, Lynn, and you are the woman I love. I shall protect you, if need be, at whatever cost to myself."

"Rafael, this is nonsense," she objected. "You don't love me at all . . . it's just infatuation you feel, and it will soon pass if only you'll allow it to." She saw the young man's usually gentle eyes kindle with protesting fire, and she added hastily, "Oh, very well — I'll tell you about Brett, though it wasn't very much, really. It was just to do with the work I'm doing on one of the paintings."

Rafael looked astounded. "It was to do with your *work*? I imagined he must have . . . how do you say it in English? . . . that he must have made a pass at you, Lynn."

"No, nothing like that."

"I am very relieved to hear it. Brett would like to make love to you, of course, but he does not dare try. You are not one of his women."

"One of his women?" she echoed faintly.

Rafael nodded. "Yes, like Juanita. She tries very hard to manipulate him, but to Brett it is all a game. But he knows that he cannot play games with you, Lynn, as he does with all the others."

Lynn closed her eyes. Rafael was completely unaware of the pain he was causing her by speaking of his brother's uncaring treatment of women. He went on now, his voice deep with concern,

"And because Brett knows you would permit no liberties, he punishes you by criticising your work. How can he be so cruel, so unfeeling?"

"No, you've got it all wrong!" she cried. "Brett had . . . he *thought* he had a good reason for blaming me, because of some damage that was done to one of the paintings."

"What damage is this?" Rafael asked, his forehead creased in a perplexed frown.

"Oh, some of the original paint had been rubbed off the canvas. It's made rather a mess, I'm afraid."

"You mean there was an accident?"

"No, not an accident. It's obvious that someone did it deliberately."

Rafael's boyishly youthful face was a picture of bewilderment. "But who would do a thing like that, Lynn? It is inconceivable, surely?"

She stared at him unhappily. How could she ever hope to make him believe that the culprit was Juanita, acting out of sheer spiteful jealousy? Anyway, what good would it do to make such an accusation?

"I . . . I can't explain," she faltered. "I don't suppose we shall ever know."

"Perhaps, after all, it was something you did yourself — a little mistake you made," Rafael suggested mildly. "But even so, it is wretched of Brett to make a big fuss . . . everyone can make a mistake sometimes. Oh, my poor Lynn . . . I am so ashamed of my brother that he can treat you in this way."

Impetuously, he reached out and drew her into his arms. Lynn, in her misery, allowed herself the comfort of being held by him, this man who was a brother of the man she loved. So like him, yet so totally unlike. Rafael was kinder, more gentle, more ready to sympathise and try to understand than Brett would ever be. For a few brief moments she could almost capture the illusion that it was Brett's lean hard body that was pressing so intoxicatingly close to hers, Brett's lips that brushed her temples with sweet caresses, breathing the tenderest words of endearment . . .

This was madness! Rafael couldn't be held to blame if he misconstrued the reason for her trembling limbs, her treacherously thudding heartbeat. She could hardly pretend that this was an innocent matter of a sympathetic man giving brotherly solace to a distressed woman. It was night, they were in her bedroom, and she wore only a thin cotton nightdress and an equally gossamer robe, her legs and feet totally bare. And Rafael vowed that he loved her! Without doubt, it was sheer insanity to permit the situation to continue a moment longer.

But even as the decision formed in Lynn's brain, there came a rap on the door. They both started in alarm, and Rafael's hold on her loosened.

"Who can it be?" he whispered.

"I . . . I have no idea!" No servant would come at this time of night, unless summoned by the bell. "Could it be Rosa-María, do you think?"

His face paled. But before he could speak there came a second knock, and a voice called, "Lynn, are you there?"

Brett!

Rafael's courage evaporated immediately. It was clear that his bravado of a few minutes ago, when he'd been so eager to confront Brett in her defense, was quite gone now that his elder brother was actually on the spot.

"What . . . what shall I do?" he asked in a panic. "He must not find me here."

She had wild hope that if she remained silent Brett would go away. But a further sharp rap disabused her of that thought.

"Lynn! Is something the matter?" Brett demanded. "Why don't you answer?"

"Just a moment," she called back, afraid that he might open the door without her permission if she didn't say something. She stared around desperately for inspiration.

"Quickly, go out on the balcony," she whispered, giving Rafael a push. "I . . . I'll send him away."

Rafael obediently did as she ordered and when the curtains had fallen back into place behind him, Lynn went to the door and opened it.

"What do you want, Brett?" she asked. "It's very late."

Now that she was standing there before him, Brett seemed curiously hesitant. His dark eyes contained a look of apology, of appeal. He began uncomfortably, "Lynn, I was pretty harsh with you earlier on. I couldn't go to bed without coming to tell you I'm sorry."

Lynn was so astonished she couldn't find her voice. Brett went on persuasively, "Look, can I come in for a minute? I want to try and explain."

"No please . . . not now!" she protested, taut with nerves. "Thank you for coming to apologise, but you can't come in."

But he was already inside, and closing the door. "I shall only stay a minute or two," he assured her. "Don't worry, there's nobody around, I made sure of that."

"But please . . . what's the point?"

"I told you, I want to explain."

"Explain what?" she asked weakly, throwing an agonised glance over her shoulder at the window.

"My whole attitude towards you," he told her. "I've done a lot of thinking this evening, and I've come to the conclusion that I may have been unfair to you in some ways."

She would dearly have liked to hear all that Brett had come to say, but she dared not let him continue with Rafael concealed on the balcony.

"Of course you've been unfair to me," she retorted, "just because I'm a woman. You regard every single one of us with nothing but contempt, fit only for taking to bed. So it really would be better if you left at once."

He shook his head, eyeing her with a curiously puzzled air.

"I admit I've held a low opinion of your sex . . . I still do for that matter. My experience of women has led me to expect them to be utterly ruthless where men are concerned."

"Oh yes, you've made that crystal clear to me," she said bitterly.

"I only wish I could take back some of the things I've said," he told her, sounding almost humble. "I've got to admit that, looking at things objectively, you haven't behaved in the same fashion as other women I've known."

"How big of you to admit that!" she hit back, her heart beating painfully. "If you're not careful, you might find yourself actually having a good word to say about me."

He took a quick step towards her. "Lynn, for God's sake don't be like this. Heaven knows I deserve it from you, but I'm trying to say I'm sorry. Can't we wipe the slate clean and begin again as though we've only just met? Couldn't you try?"

Her whole being was flaring with a wild, tumultous hope. But she dared not let him see, hardly dared even to admit to herself, the strength of her emotion. Brett couldn't really mean what he seemed to be saying, what she longed so desperately for him to mean.

Understanding none of the turmoil

within her, Brett could only see Lynn's doubt, her hesitation. He went on urgently, "Remember those times I held you in my arms, Lynn. Were they totally without meaning for you? That first time, when you fled away to your room in such a panic, was it because you hated me touching you? Or because you couldn't trust yourself if you remained a moment longer?"

A breeze, blowing more strongly then before, fluttered the long curtains at the window, jolting Lynn's mind back to the dangerous predicament she was in. Listening to Brett's impassioned words, the thought of Rafael hidden outside on the balcony had almost slipped from her mind. But suddenly she was in an agony of fear that Brett might discover his brother there.

He noticed her instinctive shiver, and said at once, "Are you cold, Lynn? There's quite a wind springing up. Let me close the windows for you."

"No!" she screamed, but silently, for the tightness of her throat allowed no sound to pass. Instead, a gasp of dismay came from the balcony.

Brett's eyes narrowed. "Is someone out there?" he demanded suspiciously. "What the devil's going on?"

In vain, Lynn tried to prevent him from striding to the window, but he brushed her aside contemptuously and flung back the curtains. The balcony wasn't large enough to afford any further concealment for Rafael, who shrank back as the light from the room fell upon him.

The two brothers stared at each other for terrifying moments of silence. When at length Brett spoke, his voice expressed the full measure of his disgust.

"If I'd had any sense, I suppose I should have expected something like this!" He swung back to Lynn, his eyes blazing. "How clever you must have thought you were — secretly enticing Rafael behind the scenes while all the time trying to make everybody believe that nothing was further from your thoughts. How many times have you entertained in your room at night, I wonder?"

"Never!" she protested huskily. "Anyway, I wasn't *entertaining* him. He just . . . just . . . "

Brett's eyes, brutal and sardonic, swept over her flimsy night attire. "I see! So my brother just happened to drop by for a chat when you were ready for bed. And naturally you let him in! God, you make me sick! I've no doubt you thought it a huge joke just now, listening to me making a complete fool of myself. But at least you've proved to me that I was right all along about women. I must have been out of my mind to even begin to think you were different from the rest."

Somehow, Rafael dredged up his courage. "Brett . . . you are misjudging Lynn," he protested. "She did not invite me to her room."

Disdainfully, Brett turned his back on Lynn and confronted his brother.

"Try not to be a bigger damn fool

than I take you for," he sneered. "Can't you see even now that she's playing you like a hooked fish on the end of a line? And what a fine catch you'd make for her!"

"You say these unkind things because you are jealous," Rafael mumbled indistinctly.

"Me! Jealous about *her*! I'm grateful, if you really want to know . . . grateful to you both for teaching me a lesson I believed I had learnt already — never, ever, trust a woman! Now get out, Rafael, and make sure you don't come back to this room, tonight or any other night. Understand?"

The younger man tried to gather together his dignity. "You cannot order me about in my own house."

"I can, and that's exactly what I'm doing," his brother said remorselessly. "You don't think I'm going to leave you here with her, do you? You're no more than a babe in arms, Rafael, when it comes to women. You just don't understand them."

"And you seriously imagine that you do?" It was Lynn who spoke, her voice charged with anger. And something deeper than anger . . . an inner need to strike out and wound him as he was wounding her. "You think everybody else is just like you . . . all taking and no giving! If that's how you *expect* other people to behave, it's hardly surprising that they often do. It's high time you learned to have a little humility, Mr. Brett Sackville, a touch less arrogance. Until you do, you'll always be as sour and bitter as you are now."

"You listen to me . . . " he began furiously, but she cut across him, storming,

"No, I won't listen to you! I've been commissioned to do certain professional work here, and I'll stay and see it through. But the job doesn't include any obligation to listen to you laying down the law. And now, if you don't mind," she finished chokily, "will you both please clear out and leave me in peace."

Frowning blackly, Brett jerked his head at his brother. "Yes, Rafael, clear out! I have a few things to make plain to Miss Forster before I leave this room."

Lynn went to the door and threw it open. "I said *both* of you, and I meant it! Will you kindly get out of my bedroom!"

A pulse throbbing at his temple, Brett scorched her with his gaze. An age went by — was it really only seconds? — before he shrugged his broad shoulders in an uncaring gesture.

"As long as we understand each other, Miss Forster," he said levelly. "And I believe we do!"

Rafael threw Lynn a helpless glance as he preceded his brother from the room. But she scarcely noticed it, too intent on being alone so that her pent-up misery could spill out. Brett claimed that he understood her, when he understood *nothing*. He would never in a hundred years allow himself to believe that she loved him, deeply and undemandingly. Brett Sackville despised her, hated her, loathed the very sound of her name. Lynn threw herself onto the bed and gave way to a storm of weeping.

# 8

BREAKFAST was never a formal meal at *La Casa de los Pámpanos* and it was the custom for people to take it whenever and wherever they chose. Lynn liked to have hers on the terrace, in a shady corner where bougainvillea tumbled over trellised arches in a luxuriant purple waterfall. She was sitting there alone the next morning, gratefully sipping strong, hot coffee after a night of little sleep, when she heard footsteps approaching. Glancing up, she saw to her dismay that it was Brett.

"Do you mind if I join you?" he asked in an even, perfectly civil tone, and Lynn could read nothing from his expression.

"No . . . no, of course not."

As he took a seat, a maidservant appeared bringing more coffee and rolls. When the girl had set them before him, Brett continued, "My mother has suggested that I should take you to the *bodega* at Sanlúcar de Barrameda this afternoon, Lynn. Did she mention it to you?"

Startled by such a suggestion coming after the scene in her bedroom last night, Lynn blurted out, "Yes she did . . . the other day. But you don't have to take me."

"Why shouldn't I?" he clipped.

She coloured. Was this another deliberate indication of the contempt he felt for her, that he could calmly propose to act as her guide as if nothing had happened?

"I . . . I can't spare the time," she evaded. "I've got to get on with repairing the damage done to Don Fernando's portrait."

"A single afternoon won't make that much difference," he pointed out. "Besides, that's hardly an explanation you could offer to my mother. She is very keen for you to see the *bodega*."

Did Señora Alejandro know anything about last night's events, Lynn wondered wretchedly. Had she and Brett quickly concocted this plan together, because she feared that her younger son was still in danger from the English girl?

"I suggest that we set out at four o'clock," Brett pressed, "when the heat of the day is passing. Would that suit you?"

It was an impossible situation, and she would be sensible to refuse. But sitting here over breakfast with him, so close that her senses were swamped by his nearness, Lynn lacked the willpower to turn down this chance of an outing with Brett.

"I . . . I suppose so," she faltered.

Her appetite had deserted her and she was unable to eat any more. She sat silently watching him through lowered lashes, while he consumed a cup of coffee and one of the warm, crusty rolls. Then he stood up, bowed to her with Spanish gallantry, and departed.

A manservant brought Lynn the two

paintings she needed as guidance for the repair work on the damaged portrait . . . a miniature of Don Fernando, and a larger painting of a family group, so she would be able to represent him fairly accurately. But she found she could do little work that morning. She constantly became aware that for minutes on end she had been staring into space, her mind relentlessly drifting into forbidden regions full of crazy, impossible dreams . . .

Brett brought his car to the front entrance at the appointed time. He looked incredibly handsome, she thought with a tightening of her heartstrings, cool and perfectly at ease in his pale fawn suit even though it was such a hot day. Lynn herself, despite the summery blue dress she wore, felt roasted by the hot sun after just a few moments in the open, and she was grateful for the car's efficient ventilation system, which sent a constant current of cool air over her as they drove.

The *manzanilla* vineyards stretched

into the distance, rolling over the undulating hills, seemingly endless. Here and there they passed a noble house or a humble cottage set alone in the countryside. And sometimes there were villages, where groups of women gossiped and giggled as they filled their big waterpots at the fountain, and sloe-eyed children played happily in the dust alongside clucking hens and scrawny dogs. The window boxes were a riot of brightly-coloured geraniums and petunias, and cool green patios could be glimpsed through fretted doorways.

"*Sol y sombra!*" Brett murmured, as they emerged from one of the villages through a shady grove of silver-leaved olive trees into the sun-parched countryside again, where bent old men were labouring between the rows of vines.

"What does that mean?" Lynn asked.

"Sunshine and shadow," he explained. "It's the everlasting story of Andalusia . . . beauty and gaiety set against the most grinding poverty. Which is why," he added, "I keep nagging Rafael about his responsibilities as an employer. But he's always happy-go-lucky, believing that as long as there's a good living for himself from the land he owns, there's nothing to worry about. Do you subscribe to that philosophy, Lynn?"

"I . . . I hardly know enough about Spain to give an opinion," she stammered, feeling confused.

"I meant as a general principal," he said sharply.

"I . . . well, naturally I think we all have to accept our responsibilities in life, and consider the wellbeing of others."

"Good!" he nodded, and lapsed into silence.

The salty tang of the sea hung over Sanlúcar de Barrameda, which was a pleasant little fishing port at the mouth of a river. Lynn caught sight of an ancient church with a beautiful Moorish doorway, and another with walls of golden stone crowned by a carved balustrade. Then they were turning through wrought-iron gates into a large courtyard lined with rows of huge casks. Climbing plants trailed in riotous profusion over archways, and Lynn caught the honeysweet fragrance of orange blossom that wafted on the air.

Brett stopped the car by the door to a small office, and got out. A swarthy-faced man came hurrying forward, sweeping off his beret and gallantly opening the door on Lynn's side.

"*Gracias*, Carlos!" said Brett with a friendly smile, and added something else in Spanish which Lynn couldn't understand.

With the heady aroma of fine wines all about her and the mass of information she was expected to absorb, Lynn became quite dizzy on her tour of the Alejandro *bodega*. The great vaulted cellars had a hushed, almost cathedral-like atmosphere. They were stacked with enormous butts of sherry in various stages of maturity, and Brett explained something about the *solera* system, the unique method of blending which made sherry a wine apart from all others. As before, in the vineyards, he seemed to get caught up in what he was telling her. Several times when Lynn was supposed to be listening she found herself just watching his face, alight with his fascination in his subject.

At the end of the tour she was made dizzier still when she was handed generous measures of the different sherries the *bodega* produced. The first one she drank down completely, but afterwards she took only a few small sips, realising how potent the wine was.

"Some people maintain that it's the sea air which gives *manzanilla* its special nutty savour," Brett told her. "I'm not convinced about that myself, but we can certainly make a type of sherry here that can't be made anywhere else."

Afterwards, he took her to a nearby café for coffee, which helped clear away the muzziness in her head. Brett sat across the table from her, his dark eyes regarding her thoughtfully.

"We might as well stay out for dinner while we're about it," he said. "There's a very good fish restaurant right down on the beach."

"Oh, but . . . "

"But what? You can't pretend there's anything special you've got to get back for."

Thinking of Juanita, she said rather desperately, "I . . . I thought *you* would probably have an engagement this evening."

"You can leave me to worry about that. So we do stay, yes?"

He was taking her altogether too much for granted! He seemed to imagine that he could rage at her one day, and the next day just snap his fingers and she'd come running.

"Look," she said rebelliously, "if this is all because you're trying to keep Rafael and me apart, there's no need. I've repeatedly told you that I have no interest in your brother except as a friend. Why won't you accept that?"

"Because I know how stubborn and pigheaded that young brother of mine can be. He insists, in his wildly exaggerated way, that he's madly in love with you and that he won't rest until he's persuaded you to marry him." Brett's brow creased into an angry frown. "It's utterly absurd!"

"Oh is it?" she demanded, stung into answering back. "Then let me tell you this. If I had the slightest wish to be Rafael's wife, I wouldn't allow *your* disapproval to stand in my way. It would be entirely a decision between Rafael and me . . . and no one else!"

"I couldn't allow that to happen," Brett said coolly.

"You couldn't stop it," she retaliated.

"Oh yes I could, make no mistake! I'd prefer to act in a reasonable, civilised way, but if you force my hand then you'll only have yourself to blame for what happens."

He looked so sure of himself, so supremely self-confident, that Lynn quailed a little before his unrelenting gaze.

"Anyway," she muttered weakly, "the question doesn't arise."

"I'm very glad to hear it. Just make sure that you don't change your mind."

Lynn stared down at the coffee in her cup, not daring to raise it to her lips for fear her trembling hands would betray her nervousness.

"Why does the possibility of having me as your sister-in-law seem so utterly unthinkable to you," she asked in a quiet voice. "Do you still believe that I'm just after Rafael's money?"

Lynn observed his hesitation. He glanced away from her, out across the café's pretty little courtyard, where fountains made dancing patterns in the amber light of the sinking sun.

"I let my anger run away with me last night," he acknowledged at last. "It was the shock of finding Rafael in your bedroom at that late hour. You must admit, it looked highly suspicious."

Her retort was quick and sharp.

"You came to my bedroom yourself. Perhaps Rafael found *that* suspicious."

"I came to apologise," he countered. "You know that . . . and so does Rafael."

"And Rafael came because he had seen how upset I was earlier on. That's all there was to it. Naturally, when somebody else knocked on my door we realised how easily the situation could be misinterpreted, and that was the only reason he hid on the balcony."

"As he took great pains to explain to me afterwards!" Brett's voice had lost its harshness and now it became gentler still. "Lynn, it's stupid for us to quarrel. As long as you understand that it would be disastrous for you to marry Rafael, and . . . "

"Thanks very much!" she cut in scathingly. "You keep implying that, and you don't seem to realise how insulting it is to me."

He looked at her incredulously. "Insulting! But why, Lynn?"

"When you're not suggesting that

I'm after your brother for his money, you hint that I'm not good enough for him."

He sighed impatiently. "All I'm saying is that you're not the right wife for Rafael, and he's not the right husband for you. He's a Spaniard, Lynn, and with his sort of personality he needs a woman who will appear to be utterly compliant to his every wish. A woman who will take a back seat in everything, yet who, from a position of apparently total self-effacement, will gently influence her husband, pushing him in the right direction. Rosa-María is exactly that sort of girl. But can you see yourself in such a role, Lynn?"

She hesitated, moistening her dry lips. "No . . . no, I suppose not. But then, I've never for a single moment imagined myself playing the part of Rafael's wife."

"Good!" Brett smiled at her, but Lynn couldn't be sure that there wasn't a tiny hint of doubt still lurking in his dark, unfathomable eyes.

"Well, now that we've cleared the air," he went on cheerfully, "I take it you won't object to having dinner with me?"

Still uncertain whether Brett was just manipulating her, simply keeping her out of his brother's path, Lynn permitted herself the luxury of giving way to her heart's longing.

"Very well!" she murmured. "Thank you, Brett."

"That's fine! It's far too early yet, of course, considering the late hours they keep in Spain. We'll stroll around a bit first."

When they emerged from the café, the evening *paseo* was beginning. Everybody in the little town, it seemed, was out for a stroll now that work for the day had finished and the cool of evening was breathing through the streets like a long sigh of relief. Giggling groups of girls dressed in their finery were longingly eyed by handsome young men very conscious of their masculine dignity, and comfortable

274

matrons paraded solemnly with their portly husbands. As the sun went down over a sea that gleamed like molten copper and the street lights came blinking on, there was a feeling of gala in the air — though a decorously formal sort of gala.

Lynn was feeling very happy because she could sense the tension dissolving between Brett and herself. They talked and laughed and altogether seemed so much in harmony that it was almost as if he could read her thoughts, for at the precise moment that Lynn realised she was hungry Brett suggested it was time they dined.

The restaurant, as he had said, stood right on the sands of the little fishing beach. It was cool and airy, yet cosy, too, with exquisite seafood served by candlelight. Far out across the dark ocean, where the lights of ships winked, hung a great silver-yellow moon in a sky that was velvet soft and studded with brilliant jewel-like stars.

They emerged at nearly midnight

and stood by a stone wall, gazing up at that romantic moon. Lynn wasn't even surprised by the gentle touch of his hand upon her shoulder, and she melted towards him as he drew her into his arms.

"Lynn!" he murmured into her hair. "Thank you for a wonderful evening."

She longed to tell him it had been wonderful for her, too, that she had never been so happy in her life before. But she was too choked with the magic of it to speak, and anyway it didn't matter — her radiance must have spoken for itself.

They remained close-for long, un-counted seconds, seeming blissfully at one. Then suddenly she felt bereft as, with a husky laugh, he released her.

"Come on, Lynn Forster, it's high time I took you home. I may *feel* like a god tonight but I'm only human, with human weaknesses, and I don't trust myself to be strong-minded for much longer."

# 9

IT was not until dinner time the next evening that Lynn learned that Brett had gone away. He had been absent at luncheon, but that wasn't unusual so she'd thought nothing of it.

Throughout the day, while trying hard to concentrate on her work, her thoughts had kept drifting back happily to the previous evening, to the meal they'd shared together in the little candlelit restaurant on the sands at Sanlúcar de Barrameda. And to those precious moments afterwards when Brett had held her in his arms and whispered against her hair until he had suddenly let her go with a joking remark, his voice husky with meaning. She had almost forgotten the faint look of doubt that still lingered in Brett's dark eyes after their quarrel was over.

Almost forgotten the harsh things he'd said to her . . .

Nothing in Brett's words or actions yesterday had given Lynn any real cause for hope. Yet, against all reason, she was filled with bright optimism. No longer did it seem insane to allow her thoughts to dwell blissfully upon him; to savour the image of his handsome, craggy face — so serious in repose, so vibrantly alive when he smiled; or to remember the feel of his arms about her, the urgent, searching pressure of his lips.

And now Brett had gone, snatching himself away from her at the moment when her hopes were riding high. He had done it once before, vanishing without warning from *La Casa Española*, in England, leaving her stranded with a feeling of emptiness and despair. Was it deliberate? To raise her up, then crush her down?

She couldn't prevent herself staring in horror across the table at Rafael, who had let out the news of his brother's departure so casually.

"I am glad that Brett has decided to stay in Cádiz for a few days," he said. "It will give me some breathing space. Believe it or not I have a list from him of things to be done on the estate which is . . . how do you say in English? — as long as your arm." He broke off and gave Lynn a concerned look. "You have turned quite pale, Lynn! Was it something I said . . . about Brett? You must not allow anything concerning him to upset you."

Lynn was aware that not only Rafael, but Señora Alejandro and Rosa-María too, were looking at her strangely. Her lips quivering, she said faintly, "You're imagining things, Rafael. I am not upset, not about anything."

Fortunately, Rafael suddenly switched his attention to his mother.

"Yesterday, *Madre*, you sent Brett to show Lynn over the *bodega*," he said reproachfully. "Surely it was my place to do this?"

"Brett is far more knowledgeable on the subject than you will ever be, Rafael," she answered dismissively. "You know that's true."

He frowned at his mother, his boyish face petulant. "Oh yes, it is always the same! Your darling Brett is so much cleverer than I am. I am never given a chance."

Señora Alejandro shot him a quick, warning glance, censuring him for speaking critically of one of the family in the presence of Lynn and Rosa-María.

"You know perfectly well that I make no distinctions whatever between my two sons. But it happens to be a fact that Brett knows a great deal more about the production of sherry than you do." She ended that aspect of the conversation by addressing Lynn. "I trust you enjoyed your visit to the *bodega*, Miss Forster?"

"Er . . . oh, yes! It was most instructive."

"You were not back for dinner,"

Rafael said accusingly. "Where were you?"

Her heart thudding, Lynn tried her best to respond in a voice that sounded suitably casual.

"Brett kindly suggested that I might enjoy going to a fish restaurant on the beach. It was very pleasant."

Again the eyes of all three were upon her. Lynn thought she could sense a kind of intrigued approval from Señora Alejandro and Rosa-María. But Rafael was frowning darkly.

"I am warning you, Lynn, do not let my brother make a plaything of you. Besides, Juanita would scratch out your eyes if she knew you had spent the evening with him."

"That is quite enough, Rafael," his mother chided him.

"But *Madre*," he protested, "everybody knows about Brett and his women. It is no secret. Juanita just happens to be the current one, that's all."

"I shall not warn you again, Rafael,"

said Señora Alejandro with controlled anger. "If you utter one more word on the subject, I shall request you to leave the table."

Like a small boy who has been reprimanded, Rafael put on a sulky expression and lapsed into silence.

The meal continued in a tense, uncomfortable atmosphere. Señora Alejandro did her best to maintain polite smalltalk, but with little success. It was an obvious relief to them all when the meal came to an end and they could disperse. Rafael made an attempt to follow Lynn from the room, but his mother called him back to say something, perhaps deliberately giving Lynn a chance to escape upstairs to her bedroom. There, she turned the key in the lock in case Rafael should be indiscreet enough to come knocking at her door again. Leaving the lights unlit, she crossed to the window and stepped outside on the balcony, but the coolness of the night air on her skin did little to alleviate the burning pain within her.

Very faintly in the hushed darkness, as if coming from far away over the Andalusian hills, she heard the strains of a guitar. And then a voice, unbearably poignant, lifted in a song of such sweet melancholy that Lynn's eyes filled with tears. Of course, it was probably just one of the vineyard workers entertaining his friends now that the day's labours were over. But to Lynn that voice, that song, seemed to epitomize the very heart and essence of unrequited love.

★ ★ ★

Several times in the following two days Rafael tried to waylay Lynn, but she flatly refused to allow him in her studio, and whenever she wasn't either there or up in her bedroom, she tried to ensure that someone else was around. Once, when she was crossing the hall, Rafael emerged from the salon and caught her arm beseechingly. A sound at the head of the grand staircase caused them both to glance up and they saw his mother looking down on them, her face set and serious. Rafael broke away in confusion, muttered something indistinct and walked rapidly away.

Lynn was trying to immerse herself in her work, determined now that just as soon as she could complete the repair to the portrait of Don Fernando and the restorative work she'd agreed to do on the other paintings, she would leave *Los Pámpanos* and return to England. She would not, could not, remain here to have her emotions toyed with by Brett Sackville, as a cat toys with a mouse. She knew now the full measure of her weakness as far as Brett was concerned. However much she might resolve not to let him undermine her defences, whenever he chose to take her in his arms and murmur soft words of endearment she would be lost . . . engulfed by that terrifying sense of longing she had come to know so well. Brett knew his power over her, and exulted in it. Her only escape lay in removing herself completely from his presence.

When at last the repair work on the damaged portrait was finished, she put the painting aside thankfully, praying that it would pass muster. The test came sooner than she expected. Not an hour later, when she was removing discoloured varnish from a picture of a nineteenth-century matador with a swirling red cape, Señora Alejandro came into the room.

"Miss Forster, I trust I am not disturbing you."

"No . . . not at all."

"I promised to come and see your work on the portrait of Don Fernando. I would have come sooner but Brett advised me against that — he said that in the early stages of restoration it is difficult for a non-professional to make a fair assessment."

"Yes, that's true," agreed Lynn, her heartbeat quickening at the thought of the denunciation that might be ahead of her. "Thank you for waiting a few days, Señora Alejandro."

She removed the painting upon her easel, and replaced it with the one in question. Then she stood back and waited with bated breath for the verdict. To her immense relief, Señora Alejandro was delighted.

"My dear Miss Forster, it looks quite magnificent! How incredible to see the colours so clear and bright, when before they were all so dark and dingy. You really are extremely clever."

"You're very kind," said Lynn, embarrassed at the unexpectedly high praise. "Of course, it still has to be revarnished."

The older woman nodded. "I am sure Brett will share my pleasure when he gets back. Just a few minutes ago I telephoned his office in Cádiz and he told me he expects to be returning late this evening."

Lynn was silent, wondering what was coming next. For clearly this would be the real purpose of Señora Alejandro's visit, not any sudden desire to see the portrait.

The señora strolled to the window and stood there gazing pensively at the sunlit grounds.

"Dear Rafael made me quite cross at dinner the other evening," she began with a rueful little sigh. "He had no justification for speaking as he did about his brother's relationships with the opposite sex. It was the grossest exaggeration, of course!"

Lynn waited silently. There was really nothing she could say. After a moment Señora Alejandro turned away from the window and their eyes met.

"Did you enjoy your outing with Brett?" Without pausing for an answer, she ran on, "There are so many delightful places for you to visit here in Andalusia, Lynn — I may call you Lynn like the rest of my family, may I not? — and you shall please call me Doña Victoria. Brett must take you to see some of the sights. I understand he will not be quite so busy from now on, having cleared up most of the backlog of work."

Lynn forced a smile. "It's a kind suggestion of yours, Doña Victoria, but I'm afraid that I myself will be too busy to take advantage of it."

"Oh, come now . . . we cannot have you working like a slave. Don't imagine I haven't noticed how, in these last two days, you've spent every daylight hour shut away in this room. Though I am grateful for such dedication, I really must insist that you have *some* relaxation. So if Brett should suggest another little outing, do please feel free to accept with a clear conscience."

So once more she was to be paired off with Brett, Lynn reflected bitterly, to protect Rafael from the danger of becoming inextricably involved with her. Of course, Doña Victoria knew that every word Rafael had said about his older brother was true — Brett was an incorrigible womanizer. And for that very reason they felt he was immune. Let Brett distract the English girl's attention, Doña Victoria must be planning, while I push Rafael into an early engagement with Rosa-María.

Politely, but insistently, Lynn said, "Thank you, Doña Victoria, but I would prefer to get my work completed so that I can return to England as soon as possible. You see, I have my future to consider."

"I am sure you have nothing to worry about in that direction, my dear . . . a young woman as charming and intelligent as you!" Doña Victoria smiled and moved towards the door. "But I will not press you any further. Perhaps Brett himself will succeed in persuading you."

As the door closed quietly behind her departing figure, Lynn felt anger and bitterness sweep over her. No doubt the clever little scheme had been hatched during that phone call to Cádiz. Brett had been summoned home by his mother to take care of a potentially dangerous situation. But they were taking too much for granted, she would refuse to co-operate . . . nothing on earth would induce her to have anything further to do with Brett Sackville. But even while her brain was making this decision, her treacherous heart was tempting her . . . she imagined herself held once more in Brett's arms, moulding the softness of her body to the lean hardness of his, yielding her lips to his . . .

The only escape was to run away, as far and as fast as she could. In three or four days, perhaps, if she worked really hard to finish her commission here, she could book herself a flight back to London. She would find sanctuary and safety in England — though not peace of mind. Lynn believed that never again would she know what it was to be at peace with herself, untormented by the memory of Brett Sackville.

Brett had not returned by the time they assembled for dinner, but then his mother had said he would be late.

Lynn felt thankful for that ... she could do again what she had done these past two nights — retire to her room the moment the meal was over.

But once she was safely upstairs, she found that no breath of wind stirred when she stepped out onto the balcony. The sky had clouded over, and the heat of the day was trapped close to the land, unable to escape into the heavens. Sitting there in an openwork basket chair, wearing nothing but the thinnest cotton frock she possessed and the bare essentials of underwear, Lynn sweltered in discomfort. She gazed down into the darkness of the garden, thinking longingly that perhaps it would be cooler by the ornamental pool where a fountain played, or in the cypress grove where the direct rays of the sun would not have penetrated all day.

On a sudden impulse, she rose to her feet and crossed to the door. Listening, she could hear no sound, and decided she could safely slip outside unobserved.

She believed she had succeeded as she gained the hall and hastened along a side corridor from which a glazed door led into the gardens. She breathed the sweet fragrance of summer jasmine and night-scented stock as she headed in the direction of the pool, guided by the soft splashing of the fountain. Sitting down on the smooth rim, she trailed her fingers in the cool, dark water. A dozen jets spurted from the mouths of unseen stone dolphins and pattered down onto floating water-lily leaves, making a blissful sound in this torrid heat. She was almost tempted to wade into the fountain's basin and allow the blessedly cool water to rain down upon her.

A sound, the scrunch of a footstep on the gravel path, made her spin round in dismay. From the darkness, she heard Rafael's voice.

"So there you are, Lynn! I saw you leave the house, but by the time I had come outside myself, you had disappeared."

Lynn could see him now, his shirt making a white splash against the darkness of the topiary hedge behind him.

"Hello, Rafael," she faltered, rising quickly to her feet. "I . . . I was just about to go back indoors."

"So soon?" He came and stood close beside her. "But you have only just come out, Lynn! Besides, there are things I must say to you."

"No, please . . . " she protested, wishing now that she'd never left the safety of her bedroom. "It's wrong for us to be alone together out here, and you know it. What would Rosa-María say . . . and your mother?"

"I do not care what they would say," he returned with dignity. "I can no longer conceal how I feel about you, *cara mía*."

He caught at her wrist, but she snatched it away.

"You're not to say things like that

to me, Rafael! I've always made it abundantly clear to you that there can never be anything between us, so why can't you accept that?"

"Because my heart will not permit me to accept it, *querida*." His voice became tragic as he went on, "If I allowed myself to accept it, then my life would not be worth living."

Lynn sighed despairingly. How was she to convince this young man who, for all his immaturity, was passionately sincere in what he believed, that there could be no future for them together? Yet it *must* be done, once and for all, leaving not the tiniest spark of hope in his heart.

"Rafael, will you kindly listen to me and not interrupt!" she began, injecting a new severity into her voice that he couldn't fail to recognise. "I shall be going away in a few days and you are not to make any attempt to follow me. Is that clearly understood?"

"But, Lynn . . . "

"No, you're not to interrupt. As I

was trying to say, I have grown very fond of you in the short time we've known each other . . . but in a purely platonic way. That's all! I want you to be happy, Rafael, truly I do. And if you want the same for me, then you must accept what I'm telling you as the truth. If you continue to talk about being in love with me you will only make me utterly wretched."

He raised his head, and in the darkness she knew he was trying to see the expression in her eyes.

"Brett is the one you love, *cara*," he said on a long sad sigh. "That is the truth, is it not?"

Her violent start of surprise must have given her away, Lynn knew, but all the same she tried to deny it.

"Me love Brett! Oh Rafael, don't be so absurd. He . . . he means nothing to me."

Ignoring her protest, Rafael went on earnestly, "Let me say this one last thing to you, Lynn . . . *because* I love you. Do not let Brett steal your heart.

295

He is my brother, and I know him so well. I warn you that if you allow it he will make use of you, play with your emotions, then cast you aside without a qualm when it suits him. That is his attitude to all women, *cara* . . . he will permit himself no deeper committment. He will break your heart if you let him."

Lynn made no further denials; it was useless. She said huskily, "When I go away from here, Rafael, I shall never see Brett again. So he will be unable to break my heart."

For a long moment they were silent, the whispering of the fountain making a poignant accompaniment to their separate thoughts. Then a door of the house opened and light spilled out across the terrace. The voice of one of the manservants called across the garden, "Don Rafael! *Dónde está usted?*"

Rafael stirred. "I am wanted, Lynn . . . I must go or he will come looking. Adios, *cara mía!*"

It was his farewell to her, Lynn knew. She made no demur when he lifted her hands to his lips in a final parting kiss. Then he rose to his feet and walked swiftly towards the house.

# 10

IT was the middle of the morning before Brett came to Lynn in her studio, but all the time, every single minute, she had been expecting and dreading the confrontation, knowing instinctively that this was the real reason for his sudden return last night.

Closing the doors behind him, he came across to her. The expression on his face was enigmatic, unreadable. Lynn couldn't hold his gaze, and glanced quickly away.

"My mother tells me she's delighted with the job you've made of Don Fernando's portrait," he began. "Clearly she doesn't suspect for one moment that it was damaged. May I see it, please?"

"Of course!"

She went to where the canvas was propped face to the wall, and turned it round. Brett studied it carefully, then nodded his approval.

"No one but an expert like yourself would know the difference, Lynn. Thank you for putting it right. I'd have hated my mother to be upset."

Lynn felt a treacherous glow of pleasure run through her veins at this compliment from him. She must steel herself against weakening in the face of any advance he made, knowing, in her heart, that she would be helpless if he really persisted.

Brett strolled across to the window, just as his mother had done yesterday. But unlike her, he perched himself casually on the sill.

"The other day I had to shoot off rather suddenly to Cádiz," he explained apologetically. "Various things had cropped up in my office there that required my being on the spot."

"Yes, Rafael told me where you'd gone."

"Rafael did?" Was there, she wondered, a slight stiffening in the arms folded across his chest? He went on, "It occurs to me, now that I have more time available, that you might like to see Cádiz, Lynn. It doesn't appeal to everyone, but I find it an attractive little town. How about this afternoon?"

Disconcerted, Lynn sought a way of escape. "But . . . but you've only just come back from Cádiz. You'd hardly want to go there again so soon."

"Why not? It's not very far, and it's a pleasant drive. Say you will." There was hidden steel in his tone.

"Thank you, but no," she said firmly, recovering her poise. "I'm afraid I'm too busy."

"But we needn't leave until about five. You wouldn't get much work done after that, would you?"

She sighed inwardly. There was no good reason why she shouldn't spare the time, and he knew it. Putting the canvas back, face to the wall, she asked shakily, "What's the real reason you're asking me out, Brett?"

There was a short silence, then

he said, "Our trip to Sanlúcar de Barrameda was quite a success, wasn't it? So I thought it would be nice for us to have another outing. Of course, there's nothing comparable to the *bodega* to show you in Cádiz . . . my warehouse there is no more than a place for storing wine that's awaiting shipment. But I'm sure we'd find something to interest you. Perhaps you'd care for a short trip in the boat."

"Boat? Which boat is that?"

"Oh, I keep a small motor yacht in the harbour there. It's useful on occasion."

The need to unseal the stopper on a new bottle of solvent gave Lynn an opportunity to appear absorbed while she fought to calm her stormy emotions. After a few moments, Brett demanded, "Well, what do you say?"

"No, I really can't, thanks all the same."

He stood up and came over to her, close enough for her skin to start prickling in anticipation of his touch. But he stopped, leaving a narrow space between them.

"Didn't you enjoy yourself the other day, Lynn?" he asked meaningfully.

"Yes, I did," she was forced to admit.

"Then why won't you come out with me again? What's so different this time?"

"Nothing," she faltered. "I just don't want to go."

"You're angry with me, Lynn," he said, frowning. "I thought you'd forgiven me for . . . well, for everything!"

It was his hesitation, his slight uncertainty that was her undoing. He was different from the arrogant, forceful personality she thought she knew. He had become human.

"Oh, I did forgive you!" she breathed.

Eagerly, he took her hand in his. "Then that's all right, Lynn! Forget this nonsense and say you'll come."

Already her senses were reeling at the mere touch of his strong brown fingers gripping her own, so slender and fragile in comparison. She did not dare look into his eyes but stared instead at the open neck of his shirt where his gold medallion hung between the dark curling hairs. A sudden longing to rest her head against his broad chest terrified Lynn with its overwhelming intensity.

Snatching her hand away, she returned to her easel and said in a husky little whisper, "All right then, I . . . I'll go to Cádiz with you, if you want me to."

"Thank you, Lynn! I'll bring the car round for you at five."

Was there a ring of cynical triumph in his voice? Or was he displaying only the normal satisfaction of a man who'd persuaded a girl to go out with him?

For the remainder of that day Lynn could not pretend she was working, even to herself. She told herself over and over again that she wasn't committed irrevocably to this date with Brett. She wouldn't even need to face him to tell him she'd changed her mind.

She could send a message by one of the servants to the effect that she felt unwell, a headache perhaps, and was remaining in her room.

But as the hours went by she sent no message. At precisely five o'clock she descended the staircase to where Brett awaited her in the hall. His look of warm approval, as he took in what she was wearing — a pleated cotton skirt that swung about her long, slender legs, and a sleeveless blouse of amber-gold silk that matched the color of her eyes — gave Lynn a warm glow of happiness. In case it should turn cold, she carried a black velvet jacket.

Their route — circuitous of necessity, Brett explained, since Cádiz lay at the end of a long spit of land — went through Jerez de la Frontera, which was a pleasant town of many churches that looked like Moorish mosques. Leaving the vineyards behind, they continued on through a chalky desert region of scrub grass and dazzling salt pans, where he pointed to a pair of eagles soaring gracefully on the rising air currents. Then they came to Puerto de Santa Maria on the coast.

"Now you've been to all three of the sherry towns," Brett told her. "It is from these, and *only* these three towns, that true sherry comes."

Catching the familiar sound of enthusiasm in his voice, Lynn smiled and said, "You could hardly be more interested in the making of sherry if you were Spanish yourself, Brett."

"Don't forget, it was we English who made it such a popular wine to drink," he replied with a laugh. "So I think a certain amount of pride on my part isn't out of place."

They spent an hour strolling round Cádiz, a city which matched Lynn's mental picture of a North African town with clustered white houses, palm trees, and noisy street markets. Brett steered her unerringly through a veritable rabbit warren of narrow back streets, which here and there opened out into a plaza with a small, dignified church.

Eventually they came to a charming shaded garden where they sat at one of the tables beneath a giant magnolia tree. A view of the sea lay before them as they sipped *manzanilla* and ate delicious prawns, with the thrumming of soft-toned guitars as a romantic background.

Lynn was aware of the potency of sherry by now, and refused more than a single glass. Even so, as they strolled in the direction of the harbour afterwards, she was glad to feel Brett's hand under her elbow. The warm sense of oneness with him, which she'd experienced at Sanlúcar de Barrameda, was returning to her now and her recent panicky distrust of him seemed exaggerated and fanciful.

Brett paused at one of the quays and pointed out his own boat, which rocked gently on the water. Lynn, admiring its sleek lines and immaculate paintwork, narrowed her eyes to read the name painted on the prow.

"Why *Dolores Silvela?*" she enquired idly.

"She was a beautiful woman I much admired," Brett replied, giving her a sideways look.

"Oh . . . oh, I see!" Lynn was angry with herself for asking the naive question and colour flamed in her cheeks.

"Dolores Silvela was a renowned *flamenco* dancer," he explained, adding with an ironic gleam in his eye, "I never actually knew her on *personal* terms, though I often saw her perform. Her grace and style impressed me greatly, so I thought it an apt name for my boat when I had it built."

It was absurd to feel such a flooding sense of relief! What difference did it make that the *flamenco* dancer hadn't actually been one of the women who had fallen under Brett's spell? There had been, and no doubt still were, plenty of others! But all the same her happy mood made her agree eagerly when Brett suggested they go aboard for a short trip.

The *Dolores Silvela* was as beautifully

appointed inside as it was immaculate outside. Starting the powerful engine, Brett cast off and they nosed neatly through the lines of other boats until they reached the open sea. When he opened the throttle the boat responded at once, surging through the grey-green water with a lift of its prow, leaving a long foamy wake behind.

Cádiz, as they receded from it, became more and more beautiful, the clear atmosphere sparkling with such radiance that Lynn could understand when Brett told her that the city was sometimes called 'the cup of silver.' Farther out, when the Spanish coastline had diminished to a long low smudge on the horizon and the northern tip of Africa had made its mysterious appearance as a grey silhouette of distant mountain peaks, Brett eased the engine to a stop, letting the *Dolores Silvela* gently ride the miniature waves. Away to the west, the sun dipped lower over the sea until the whole western sky was a magnificent blaze of fire, a raging inferno of orange and yellow and deep, sullen red, smoking like some awesome volcano. Time seemed to have come to a stop and the world stood still.

"Oh Brett!" she breathed in fascinated awe. "I've never, ever seen a sunset to equal this. It . . . it's all so vast, it makes you feel insignificant. Just a tiny speck in all this great immensity."

He was standing beside her at the rail and, almost unnoticed, his arm had crept around her. His hold tightened a little now, and he drew her closer. They stayed thus, scarcely speaking, until at last the sun went down in a final burst of glory. Then swiftly, with the brief dusk of these southern latitudes, the daylight faded into velvet night.

Still they stayed unmoving, his arm about her. Then, slowly, he drew her round to face him and, cupping her chin between his hands, he leaned forward and kissed her lightly on the forehead. With featherlight gentleness his lips moved over her face, touching her temples, her eyes, her cheek, the soft hollows of her throat, and finally came to rest warmly on her mouth. She gave a deep, soundless sigh and melted against him.

"Lynn, oh Lynn, you're so beautiful," he murmured as he broke away. Then he added reluctantly, "I'm afraid we're breaking all sorts of rules, riding without navigation lights. I'd better go and switch them on."

Lynn felt bereft when he left her to go to the wheelhouse. The moment had been magical, and she had wanted Brett to go on kissing her for ever and ever, loving her . . . Then as the green and red lights flashed on, she snapped back to a state of reality, and realised how vulnerable she was at this moment. She called shakily, "Hadn't we better be heading for shore now?"

Brett reappeared, his splendid body a dark silhouette against the paler darkness of the sky.

"Not yet, surely?" he said. "There's no rush, Lynn. I know, I'll open a bottle of wine . . . there'll be some in the fridge."

"No," she said nervously. "No more wine. I've had enough already."

"Some fruit juice, then," he suggested. "And I expect I could rustle up some food. What do you fancy?"

"Nothing to eat, thanks. Just fruit juice."

Brett brought two glasses up on deck, and they sat side by side on one of the hatches, his arm around her again, their eyes turned to the fairyland of distant lights that marked the shore. When his fingers traced a tingling line down the skin of her arm, she shivered ecstatically. To try and cover his effect on her, she said quickly, "It's getting chilly. Shouldn't we be getting back now?"

Brett hesitated, as if about to argue, then said with a shrug, "As you wish, Lynn."

Again she felt that curious sense of coldness when he left her to go to the wheelhouse. She heard the starter motor whirr, there was a splutter and a cough from the engine, then silence. Brett tried again, without success, and then again. Finally, Lynn went to the door and peered in at him.

"What's the matter?" she asked anxiously. "Why won't it start?"

"I wish I knew!" Brett fiddled with various controls and then tried yet once more, to no avail. Checking one of the dials on the instrument panel, he exclaimed, "Of all the damn fool things! We're out of fuel, Lynn. I just didn't think to check."

"Are you sure?" she asked suspiciously. "I mean, don't you carry an emergency supply?"

Brett shook his head regretfully. "I'm afraid not."

"Then what are we going to do?" she demanded, feeling a wave of panic break over her. "There must be something you can suggest."

"There is!" he replied calmly. "We sit tight and wait. It's perfectly safe, Lynn . . . we're not on a shipping lane here, and if something else does chance to come along, we're carrying proper lights. All we've got to do is hang about for the fishing boats to return with their catch. I'll signal, and one of them will give us a tow."

"When will that be?" she asked, partially reassured.

"Oh, first light or soon after."

"First light?" She almost screamed at him in her dismay. "But that's hours away."

"There's no need to make a fuss," he reproved. "Things aren't all that bad, Lynn. We've got shelter and warmth in the cabin, and food and drink. And," he added with an encouraging smile, "we've got each other."

She took a step back from him, and found herself pressing against the rail.

"Look," she said furiously, "if you expect that . . . "

"I don't expect anything, Lynn!" His voice was soft, coaxing. "I'm merely suggesting that since we've got to spend the next few hours in each other's company, there's no reason why we shouldn't make them as pleasant as possible."

In that moment she almost hated Brett. All the helpless, hopeless love she had felt for him all this time vanished with lightning speed at the frightening look of determination in his dark eyes. Her only wish now was to escape from him, but with miles of dark empty sea surrounding the drifting boat there was no chance of that. Unless . . . with her eyes Lynn measured the distance to the cabin. If she could slip inside before he guessed her intention and lock the door she would be safe.

Darting forward, she scrambled down the short companionway, burst into the cabin and slammed the door shut behind her. But she found to her dismay that the key was not in the lock. There were no bolts, either . . . no way of securing the door against Brett if he decided to follow her.

Which he immediately did. Lynn heard his footsteps cross the deck and descend the stairway ... deliberate, unhurried. With a feeling of utter helplessness she watched as Brett pushed open the cabin door and came in. For a moment he stood there looking at her with hostile eyes. Then, thrusting a hand in his trouser pocket, he took out a key and tossed it on the table.

"It rather spoilt your little game, didn't it, my dear Lynn, me having the key?"

"You took it deliberately, didn't you?" she accused him. "You'd got it all worked out in your mind."

Brett shrugged, and didn't try to deny that. Instead, he said with a hint of sarcasm, "Must you keep up this absurd pretence? You seem to overlook the fact that I've held you in my arms several times now and felt how your body reacts to me. The chemistry works for both of us, Lynn, it works in a big way! So how about burying our differences and accepting each other for what we really are?"

"Go away," she said huskily. "If you had the tiniest spark of decency you'd keep out of this cabin and let me have it to myself."

"And waste an opportunity that might not occur again? Be reasonable, Lynn. You must long ago have given up all hope of ensnaring me in your feminine spider's web . . . you've got your sights set on an easier target now. So why not drop the big act of outraged virtue and be your true self for once?"

"Just get out and leave me alone," she cried, in a voice that was tense with loathing.

"Not until I've forced an honest admission out of you," he said, his jaw tightening. He came towards her across the narrow cabin, and there was no escape. The next moment Lynn found herself pinioned against his hard, lean body — a helpless prisoner in his arms. His mouth came down on hers in a crushing kiss that seemed devoid of tenderness, a passionate, bruising kiss that demanded a response.

And, dismayingly, she felt herself responding, just as Brett so arrogantly expected her to. With a desperate effort of will, she fought against her own intense longings and tried to push herself away from him. But Brett held her there with contemptuous ease, lifting her in his arms and laying her down on the cushioned settee that ran along one wall. Then, quickly, he lowered himself on top of her. His hands began to caress her, his fingers stroking the soft flesh beneath her thin clothing, moulding themselves around her thighs, her hips, and rising up to cup the smooth warm curves of her breasts.

Lynn somehow summoned up fresh strength, and she arched her body away from his in a last frantic attempt to drive him off, pushing against his chest with all her might. Her fingers caught in the open neck of his shirt and the cotton fabric ripped in her hand. Brett laughed exultantly and tore off the garment, tossing it aside. In the soft light of the bulkhead lamps his bare, suntanned torso gleamed with sweat, and the medallion swung free on its slender golden chain.

"So you can't wait, my darling?" he said huskily. "But you like to play it rough, don't you? Is that what your acting has all been for?"

In a daze of horror, Lynn felt his fingers at the neck of her silk blouse, dragging the buttons apart with impatient haste. She went utterly limp, lying back and staring up at him with eyes that sparked with hatred.

"I can't fight you any more, Brett," she whispered helplessly.

He was triumphant. "So you admit that you want me?"

"No, no! I never will. But I haven't the strength to fight you . . . you'd always get your own way. So rape me if you must . . . if that's the kind of man you are."

Suddenly, Brett's hands were still. He released his hold on her and stood up. His dark eyes were smouldering with fury as he glared down at her.

"That was a filthy thing to say. By God, you've got a spiteful tongue!"

Free of him at last, free of his crushing weight, Lynn found her fear receding and her anger rising. Anger that was mingled with a sense of despair because, in these last lust-filled moments, he had destroyed her deep down, secret hopes.

"How can you accuse *me* of spite," she cried, "when everything you do is motivated by spite and hatred against women? Just because a few of us have fallen short of an absurdly idealized image you've got in your head, you seem intent on proving that every single member of my sex is despicable. You're insane! Just suppose that, because I've had the misfortune to meet you, Brett Sackville, I were to write off every single man in the world as just as vicious and ... and as steeped in depravity as you are!"

She flinched, panic gripping her

again, because for a moment he looked dangerous, as if he really wanted to strangle her.

"You as much as accused me of intending to rape you," he muttered in a choked voice.

"Well, isn't it true? Isn't that exactly what you've been planning since you first suggested bringing me to Cádiz? You had it all cleverly worked out, didn't you . . . getting me on your boat and then pretending to run out of fuel — because that's all a pretence, isn't it?"

He didn't deny a word of her accusation. His voice was like the rasping of stone upon stone. "I have never in my life made love to an unwilling woman."

"You misuse the word *love*!" she returned scornfully. "It sounds dirty on your lips."

"You know what I mean," he rapped back. "I honestly believed that you were willing . . . more than willing! *If I was wrong*, then I apologise — for that and for that only!"

Wearily, Lynn rose to her feet and smoothed down her crumpled dress. Swaying slightly, she stood with her hands pressed to her burning forehead.

"Please, let's get back now," she said faintly.

He shook his head. "I told you, we're here until dawn."

She stared at him, bewildered. "But what's the point, now? You're not persisting with that ridiculous story about having no fuel?"

He returned her gaze without expression. "We're here until dawn," he repeated, "and that's final!"

"But why? Give me one good reason."

"With pleasure!" His face twisted into a sardonic smile. "You see, my dear Lynn, when we return to *Los Pámpanos* tomorrow, although you and I will know that in fact nothing happened tonight . . . well, *almost* nothing, no one else will think so."

"They will when I tell them," she

replied furiously. "I'll make that very clear."

"And don't you think it will strike them that the lady doth protest too much? Just consider . . . you voluntarily go off for the evening with a man whose reputation as far as women are concerned is . . . shall we say *considerable*, and of which fact you are perfectly well aware. You put out to sea with him alone, in his boat, and you arrive back next morning having spent the night aboard. What inference would you yourself draw from such a situation?"

"You . . . you're utterly contemptible!" she whispered on a fading breath. "What possible purpose will it serve, to destroy my reputation in the eyes of your family? In a few days I shall be gone."

"But I'm determined to put an end once and for all to this romantic nonsense about you that has been filling Rafael's head. My brother needs protecting from himself! When he sees

Lynn Forster in her true colours — and they *are* your true colours, aren't they? — he will quickly abandon his childish infatuation and turn his attentions where they truly belong . . . to Rosa-María."

"And to achieve that end," she whispered incredulously, "you would ruin me in your brother's estimation?"

"If what you insist is true and you are not interested in Rafael, then his good opinion cannot matter to you one way or the other."

"Of course it matters! I don't want *anyone* to think badly of me."

"Then I'm afraid," he rejoined ironically, "you'll just have to put up with it. And now I suggest that we both get some sleep."

She looked at him beseechingly. "Please take me back, Brett. I swear to you that I never have, and never will in the future, do *any*thing to encourage Rafael in the slightest way."

He shook his head. "Not good enough! You've promised that in the past, but it hasn't done anything to deter Rafael. No, I'm afraid you won't alter my decision, Lynn, so I shouldn't waste your breath trying. You'll find blankets in the locker over there."

His eyes were flint hard and she knew it was useless to appeal to his better nature — because he had none. She murmured anxiously, "And . . . where will you . . . ?"

His laugh cut into her like a whiplash.

"Oh, you don't need to worry about where I shall sleep! You can feel quite confident that any desire I might have had to spend the night with you has completely evaporated. So you may sleep safely in the knowledge that frozen virtue has triumphed. I'll bid you goodnight, Miss Lynn Forster, and go up on deck in search of some fresh air. It has suddenly become unbearably oppressive down here."

Fishing a thick knit sweater from a locker, he pulled it over his head. Then, without a backward glance at her, he opened the door and vanished up the companionway.

Lynn stood tensely still, listening. But he made no sound on the deck above and she could hear only the waves slapping gently against the hull. And once, far off, the echoing call of a ship's siren. It was a sound of utter desolation.

# 11

LYNN doubted that she managed to get any sleep at all, certainly she was wide awake when the first steely light of dawn crept into the cabin. She had lain on the bunk fully dressed, and now she got up and moved stiffly to the door. There was no more fight in her. She just wanted to bring this horrible charade to as swift an end as possible.

She found Brett in the wheelhouse, crouched on a benchlike seat, a reefer jacket pulled around his shoulders. In sleep, his features in repose, he looked quite harmless — almost vulnerable — and it was difficult for Lynn to equate him with the man who had so cruelly attacked her last night. As she stood watching him, Brett's eyes opened and he sat up, stretching and yawning.

"It's dawn," she pointed out in a crisp voice. "Can we please get going now?"

He shook his head. "Not for a little while. If you're hungry, help yourself to whatever there is."

Though Lynn hadn't eaten a full meal since lunch-time yesterday, the very thought of food made her stomach heave.

"But why can't we go?" she demanded. "What's the point of waiting any longer?"

He didn't answer, but stood up and went out on deck to the rail.

"Listen!" he said. "Can't you hear them?"

To Lynn, everything seemed still and silent in this vast emptiness. The water was very calm, like stretched gray silk, veiled with a tenuous morning mist. Then, very faintly, from a long way off, she heard a low steady chugging sound.

"The fishing boats," Brett explained, in answer to her enquiring look.

"They'll be reaching us in about fifteen minutes or so."

"But . . . but there's no reason to wait for them now. You've admitted you've got fuel."

"I've admitted nothing," he returned calmly. "Let's make some coffee, you look as if you need some. Didn't you sleep well?"

"Did you expect me to?"

He shrugged, and went down to the cabin. She remained on deck, staring into the mist, trying to discern the outlines of the returning fishing boats. As she watched, the Eastern sky took on a faint rosy hue, then glittering shafts of golden light struck heavenwards until, as the sun lifted itself above the horizon, the whole sea and sky blazed gloriously. Caught up in such beauty, Lynn almost forgot where she was, until Brett's voice brought her back to cold reality.

The steaming coffee he gave her was a welcome restorative. By the time she'd finished drinking it, the fishing boats were in sight . . . no more than large dinghies, she saw, painted yellow and with curiously raised prows. In response to Brett's wave, one of them changed course slightly and drew alongside.

There were five men altogether in the boat. They stared at Lynn curiously, not grasping the situation, until Brett spoke to them in rapid Spanish. Lynn couldn't understand a word he said, but her cheeks flamed when she saw the fishermen exchange knowing looks, nudging each other and guffawing.

"What are you telling them?" she whispered fiercely.

"Just giving them the picture," he replied easily, and continued talking in Spanish. A swarthy young man of about her own age was staring in openmouthed envy, and one of the older men gave her a lascivious wink. He made a loud comment to his companions which, judging from their hilarious reaction, was probably obscene. Lynn could stand no more.

She turned tail and fled to the concealment of the cabin, shutting herself from their sight. But even with the door closed, she could not shut out the sound of their ribald amusement. She sat crouched down on the settee and covered her ears with shaking hands, and wished she were dead. It was despicable of Brett, unforgivable, to treat her like this. But nothing he could do now was worse than what he had already done. The man was utterly vile.

After a few minutes, the fishing boat's engine roared into life again, and Lynn felt a gentle tug as the *Dolores Silvela* began to move through the water. They were under tow. Once at the quay, she had perforce to run the gauntlet of the fishermen's sly looks. A group of wives, full-skirted and black-shawled against the morning chill, awaited their menfolk, and Lynn felt mortifyingly conspicuous in her thin cotton dress.

The drive back to the Alejandro estate

through the awakening countryside was made in almost total silence. Brett offered to stop somewhere for breakfast, but she still had no appetite. As they entered the house, three servants were in the hall, cleaning and polishing before the family were about. They gazed at the pair covertly, murmuring "*Buenos días*" respectfully. But Lynn was painfully aware that the moment she and Brett were out of earshot the gossip and speculation would begin.

She left Brett at the head of the curving staircase. Once safely inside her room, Lynn collapsed thankfully upon the bed. Yet, curiously, she remained dry-eyed. She felt drained of emotion, numbed by the thought of the hours and days of bitter humiliation that lay ahead, the months and years of empty despair in store for her when she returned to England.

For more than an hour she did not stir. Then, wearily, she levered herself up from the bed. Absorption in work was an anodyne, she had discovered, though never before had she needed balm for such a savage bruising of her heart and mind. After a bath, she donned her working clothes, then slipped furtively through the empty corridors into her studio. Through determination and strict mental discipline, she made some slight progress . . . it was a Godsend, at least, that such meticulous work demanded her undiluted attention.

Taken by surprise, she glanced over her shoulder guiltily as the door opened. Rafael entered, his boyish good-looks marred by a censuring black frown.

"Lynn, I have heard! How could you do this thing?"

She stared at him in bleak dismay, still unprepared for the onslaught despite all her attempts to ready herself.

"I . . . I don't know what you mean, Rafael," she faltered.

"You know very well what I mean! You spent the night with Brett on his boat. You cannot deny it."

Lynn made a pathetic attempt to resume working, but at once realised that she might easily do some damage in her present state of agitation. She stopped, and looked again at Rafael.

"It was merely a matter of running out of petrol," she explained, aware that the wavering of her voice made it sound horribly unconvincing.

"Brett does not do such a careless thing," he replied with an impatient gesture. "Lynn, I am . . . I am *shattered* that you could behave in such a way! I believed with my whole heart that you were quite different from all those other women of my brother's. And now you have proved me an idiot — an innocent, trusting fool."

"Oh Rafael, you've got it all wrong," she said, with a catch in her breath. "Between Brett and I . . . well, nothing *happened*! We just had to wait until the fishing boats came back at dawn. I spent the night in the cabin, and Brett in the wheelhouse."

"I am expected to believe this?"

Rafael said sorrowfully. "I *know* my brother . . . I have witnessed the magnetism he exerts over woman. I have seen the longing in their eyes when they look at him . . . I have even seen it in your own eyes, Lynn. But I thought that, unlike the others, you had the strength of will and moral purpose to resist such temptation."

"Stop it, Rafael!" she cried despairingly. "You're being unfair."

He dismissed her protest with a look of scorn. "I warned you myself, more than once, of the cavalier way in which Brett treats women. Yet you were perfectly willing to go out with him for the evening . . . you agreed to go with him, alone, for a trip in his boat and — if I am to believe any part of what you say — you readily accepted his word for it when he pretended there was no fuel, and said that you must spend the night with him! I beg you, Lynn, credit me with a little intelligence."

She stared at Rafael miserably. It was

working out exactly as Brett had so cynically forecast. His reputation with women ensured that no one would ever believe that their night together had been spent innocently.

"I have told you the truth, Rafael," she insisted, with a feeling of desperation.

"No you have not," he said sadly. "It is quite impossible for me to believe that Brett would have an attractive girl like you virtually his for the taking, and not avail himself of the opportunity. If you told me he had done so, if you admitted you had finally succumbed to my brother's overwhelming persuasions, I think I could still have found it in my heart to forgive you, Lynn."

The tears that, in her bedroom, had remained unshed threatened to blind her now. So be it, she thought with an ache of despair . . . Brett's plan had worked, and his young brother's adoration of her was at an end. That much good, at any rate, had resulted from her degradation.

"The question of your forgiveness

does not arise, Rafael," she said in a choked, lost voice. "I have told you how I feel about you, and that could never have changed. Go to the girl who loves you, and forget about me."

"Forget you!" he exclaimed, spreading his hands in a helpless gesture. "I could never do that, Lynn . . . your memory will be engraved upon my heart forever. The pain of what you have done will never depart."

"I think it will," she returned bitterly. "Now please go away, Rafael, and leave me in peace. There is no point in us talking any more."

For several long moments he stood gazing at her, his dark eyes clouded with sorrow. Then, with another helpless shrug, he turned away and left the room.

Lynn would dearly have liked to skip luncheon, but she knew that the confrontation with Brett's mother had to be gone through sometime, and she decided it was best to get it over with. To her dismay, everyone was assembled in the dining-room when she went in, including Brett himself, and they all turned to stare at her. Doña Victoria nodded coolly and Rosa-María, engrossed in an animated conversation with Rafael, gave Lynn a nervous smile that conveyed an equal measure of censure and pity. Rafael pointedly avoided speaking to her, and it was only Brett who did not seem ill-at-ease as they all took their places around the table.

Lynn couldn't help noticing that Rosa-María, who always sat beside her, was placed a little farther away today, and she wondered bitterly if Doña Victoria had given specific instructions to the servants about this before they laid the table. As a tainted woman, she must not be permitted to infect the innocent young Spanish girl who was now virtually assured of becoming Rafael's wife!

Already, things seemed to be moving quickly in that direction. Within a few minutes, Rafael announced from his place at the head of the table that he was thinking of going to Seville the next day.

"Some friends of mine, Francisco and Paulina Fabie, are always pressing me to go and visit them in their new apartment. I was wondering, Rosa-María, if you would care to accompany me?"

The girl's sloe-black eyes lit up with pleasure, but before answering she flashed a timidly questioning glance at Rafael's mother. Doña Victoria's smile endorsed the suggestion with wholehearted approval.

"It is most desirable, my son, that you should keep in touch with friends you made at University, and naturally Francisco's wife will want to meet Rosa-María. I met Paulina once, if you remember, and I am sure the two girls will get on famously together."

It doesn't matter to anyone now whether I'm here or not, Lynn thought suddenly. The problem her presence had created for Brett and his mother had been finally overcome, and Rafael was safely out of her 'clutches.' Brett would have no further reason for insisting that she remain at *Los Pámpanos* until the commission she had undertaken was completed . . . she could leave any time she chose. Lynn's sense of professional integrity would oblige her to finish the painting she was currently working on — which fortunately needed only a few more hours — but the remainder could be handed over to any competent Spanish restorer.

Her mind almost made up, Lynn happened to meet Brett's eyes across the table. In the instant before she glanced hastily away she seemed to read something in them that was different from the harsh triumph of a few hours ago. In their dark depths a question lurked . . . perhaps, she thought with a flutter of panic, he was considering whether she had yet suffered enough, or whether he could tighten the screw another turn or two. If he guessed that she intended to leave *Los Pámpanos*, he might try to prevent her — from sheer vindictiveness!

Her resolution hardened. She would slip away from the house unobserved. She would be aboard a plane for England before Brett so much as missed her.

But how to arrange it? That was the difficulty.

There was one person here who might be willing to help her, Lynn decided. She believed that there was compassion in Rosa-María's heart which could be appealed to.

When the dreadful luncheon had dragged its way to an end and they were all rising from the table, Lynn whispered to Rosa-María, "There's something I'd like to ask you. Could we talk privately?"

"Oh Lynn, I do not know ... " Rosa-María was clearly embarrassed, but her essential kindness prevailed and she added quickly, "*Sí sí*, if you wish! I will come as soon as I can."

Lynn had to wait impatiently for more than half an hour before she heard a muffled tap on the door. Rosa-María stepped hastily into the room as though she were doing something frightful.

"If Rafael or his mother knew I was here with you, they . . . they would not like it," she began uneasily.

"I shan't tell them," Lynn assured her. Then, "You think badly of me, don't you, Rosa-María?"

The girl bit her lip. "I have no right to make a judgment of you, Lynn. It is not my concern."

Lynn felt a fierce urge to explain exactly what had happened on the boat, to clear herself of blame in Rosa-María's eyes. But it was pointless — foolish even, if she wanted the Spanish girl's help. So she merely said, "Always remember, Rosa-María, that there are two sides to every question. Don't condemn me utterly."

"I . . . I do not condemn you, Lynn," she protested. But those soft dark eyes told another story. Rosa-María's conventional Spanish upbringing was shocked beyond understanding.

Lynn said quickly, persuasively, "Will you help me to get away from here, please, without the others knowing?"

Rosa-María drew back, clearly alarmed. "But how can I do that?"

"Easily! The difficulty for me is in not being able to speak Spanish. I want to book a seat on the first possible flight to London, and I need a taxi to pick me up and take me to the airport. But it mustn't come right up to the house, you understand? I just want to slip away unnoticed. It's the best thing."

The girl still looked doubtful, and Lynn pressed, "You could do everything on the telephone, Rosa-María. Please say that you'll help me. I can't stay here, not the way things are."

There was a lengthy pause, then she nodded her head. "I will do my very best, Lynn. I will return later and tell you what I have been able to arrange."

There was another agonised period of waiting. Lynn knew it was useless to try and work until Rosa-María returned. At long last there were footsteps outside and the girl slipped into the room with the same air of guilt as before.

"Here, Lynn, it is all written down for you. Tomorrow morning early, you see . . . you must change planes at Barcelona. The taxi will await you at the gates at six o'clock. You must ask for your ticket at the airport departure desk."

Lynn smiled at Rosa-María gratefully.

"I can't thank you enough. Try to believe me, I do sincerely wish you every happiness with Rafael. I . . . I never wanted him for myself."

"It was Brett you wanted all the time . . . I know that." Rosa-María's eyes were pensive, clouded with distress. "But you have lost all hope with Brett now. Oh, I can understand the temptation when a man pleads, but it is only if you are steadfast in refusing him that he will respect you. And there is no love in a man's heart without respect, Lynn. You must know that to be true."

There was no point in argument, in denials. Lynn said hurriedly, "This will be goodbye then, Rosa-María. I shall not come down to dinner this evening . . . will you make an excuse for me? And tomorrow, after I am gone, please tell Doña Victoria that I was sorry to leave without informing her, but I felt it was the best way. I am sure, in the circumstances, she will agree with me."

"Very well, Lynn. If that is what you wish, I will tell her."

Lynn felt no animosity towards Doña Victoria. She had fought for what she truly believed was best for her son. But Lynn knew, without doubt, that although she had welcomed Brett's help in turning Rafael's affections away from her and back to Rosa-María, Doña Victoria would never have stooped to being an accessory in that final, loathsome trick of his.

Brett, and he alone, was unscrupulous enough to carry out something so despicable. At least, Lynn thought with an overwhelming sense of relief, she would never have to set eyes on Brett Sackville again.

But she was to be proved wrong.

In the evening, after completing work on the matador painting and gathering up all her equipment, Lynn retired to her bedroom. At her request, the maid brought her a light supper on a tray, just an omelette and a glass of cool white wine. This eaten, Lynn set about packing her things, and when it was done she went to the balcony and stood gazing out into the darkness.

Rafael had been quite right in one respect . . . Andalusia had undoubtedly cast its magic spell upon her, Lynn thought with an aching sense of sadness. To the end of her days she would carry with her a picture of its perpetually blue skies and blazing sunshine; its velvet nights spiced with a hundred fragrant scents;

its hardworking, happy people who sang with simple joy when work was done.

How she wished she could have been here to see the harvest. But she would never return to Spain. She could never come back to this country that had brought her so much pain and anguish.

A tap on her door brought Lynn back to the present. Thinking it must be Rosa-María with some further message about her journey, she crossed swiftly to the door and opened it. Brett stood there. He at once moved to come in, but Lynn stood firm, barring his path.

"What . . . what do you want?" she faltered.

"You weren't at dinner tonight," he said accusingly.

"No, I . . . I didn't feel like coming down. Surely I have that choice?"

"Of course! But from what Rosa-María said I thought perhaps you were feeling unwell."

"As you can see, I am perfectly well," she returned. "But I *am* tired, so if you will excuse me . . . "

She tried to close the door but Brett gripped the handle and prevented her.

"Must you take it so badly? Surely you can see now, looking back, that I had to do what I did?"

"Including," she demanded with bitter irony, "making a bid to rape me?"

"Lynn, for God's sake!" Brett glanced over his shoulder. "I can see you're in no fit state to think straight yet. We'd better talk about it again tomorrow."

Tomorrow . . . tomorrow she would be gone.

"As you wish," she said coldly, seizing her chance to get rid of him. And firmly closing the door in his face, she turned the key in the lock.

Hidden from Brett's sight, her brief flare of defiance died and she sank wearily onto the bed. Far into the night she still lay awake, trembling and weak, a prey to soul-bruising thoughts.

# 12

IT was still dark outside when Lynn roused herself. Heavy eyed and weary, she washed, then put on the clothes she'd laid out in readiness. Everything else was packed.

With utmost care, she opened her door and peered out into the corridor. The house seemed silent and nobody stirred. Laden with her suitcase and equipment box, and carrying her shoes too, she made her way as quickly as possible down the curving staircase and across the hall to a small side door. Slipping her shoes on, she let herself out into the first pallid light of early morning and headed briskly for the gates.

She had a long wait for the car, and wished she'd thought to ask Rosa-María to arrange for it to come earlier. But at least she was clear of the house now . . . leaving any later she would have run the risk of being seen by the servants. Lynn just wanted to vanish, without the need for any explanations to anyone.

The taxi driver was, fortunately, a taciturn man and merely grunted "*Buenos días*" as he took her luggage from her, asking no questions. As the car drove off, Lynn allowed herself a long, last look at *La Casa de los Pámpanos*. In the early sunlight, against a sky shot through with the iridiscence of mother-of-pearl, the tiled roof glowed a warm reddish-brown and the white walls echoed the pale hues of the vaulted heavens. A straggling skein of wild geese was just passing over the great house, heading for the lonely marshlands of the Guadalquivir delta.

A lump came into Lynn's throat and tears misted her eyes. She turned away abruptly and stared ahead of her — she *must* think of the future. But the prospect before her was bleak and empty, with no light beckoning to her from the end of the long dark tunnel.

* * *

At London airport, Lynn was greeted by cold blustery rain. She refused a taxi and caught the service bus to the air terminal in order to conserve her limited funds. She hadn't, she realised, even presented a bill for her services. Tomorrow she'd have to set her mind to ways of earning more money, but just at the moment she could only think of reaching home . . . of buying what food she needed at the shop on the corner, and shutting herself away with her misery.

The flat smelt stale and musty. She threw open a window and at once had to shut it again to keep the wind and rain from blowing in. She stood there for several minutes, staring out at the grey street, at the people hurrying past hunched under their umbrellas.

Desolately, Lynn wondered if she

would ever see or hear from Brett again. Sooner or later he would be returning to England and spending much of his time here in London. But it was unlikely, in this teeming city, that their paths would ever cross. They moved in altogether different worlds. Brett would never frequent the coffee bars and inexpensive cafés that suited Lynn's tight budget . . . he would never leap on crowded buses and clamber aboard jampacked tube trains. Perhaps, she thought, uncaring about the money involved, he would feel obliged to pay her for the work she'd done at The Spanish House in Sussex. But even if this occurred to him, he would only instruct his secretary to deal with the matter, then promptly dismiss it completely from his mind — and Lynn Forster along with it.

Sustained only by cups of tea, not having eaten since that last supper tray at *Los Pámpanos*, she became curiously lightheaded as the day wore on. Her mind kept drifting into daydreams and she pictured Brett not as the monster she knew him to be, but as the perfect, ideal lover. She remembered that day on the beach when she'd hurt her ankle . . . the care with which he'd carried her in his arms, his tender solicitude, the feather kiss he had dropped on her hair — no, she had surely not imagined that . . .

At long last the grey daylight faded into dusk — a slow drawn-out twilight unlike the swift nightfall she had become used to in Andalusia. Lynn sat on, unmoving, preferring the creeping shadows to the harsh reality of electric light.

The doorbell pealed peremptorily, and then pealed again — a strident, impatient sound. Lynn dragged herself to her feet, hardly even curious about who it might be.

When she opened her front door, the figure standing silhouetted against the light of the hallway looked tall and menacing.

"Lynn! What the devil did you think

you were up to, rushing away like that without a word to anyone?"

"Brett!" she gasped. "What . . . what are you doing here?"

Brusquely, he pushed past her into the flat, switching on lights as he went. In the living-room he stood staring around him, taking in the three cups and saucers which had accumulated, the undrawn curtains, the crushed cushions on the chair in which she'd been sitting for so long. Then his relentless gaze swept over her, noting every detail of her dishevelled appearance.

"I expected you to stay until you'd finished the job you were commissioned to do, Lynn. It simply didn't occur to me that you might sneak away like that."

"Why should I stay on and be even more humiliated?" she said wearily. A sob broke in her throat. "You've achieved what you set out to do, so why can't you leave me alone now? Why can't you leave me in peace to try and forget the whole wretched affair — not that I shall ever be able to forget it as long as I live."

His belligerence faded at once and he looked at her apologetically.

"I'm sorry, Lynn, I never expected . . . I never intended you to feel so badly about what happened. That was what I wanted to say to you when I came to your room last night. You see, at first I really did believe I was dealing with a girl who had no feelings to *be* hurt. Or rather, to be honest, that's what I'd always been intent on proving to myself."

"Proving . . . ?" she faltered. "I . . . I don't understand what you mean."

He took a step closer, and she shrank back from him.

"I'd firmly got it into my head," he explained, "that, like all the other women I'd known, you were only out for what you could get where men were concerned. And I was determined to show you that you couldn't win with me . . . that I'd take what I

354

wanted, when I wanted, with no strings attached! That first evening on the patio at *La Casa Española*, I thought I had demonstrated that fact to you."

"You did!" she said huskily, with a shudder of remembrance. "I got the message!"

"I intended to show you that if you chose to play the feminine game of making yourself seductive, you'd get more than you bargained for. Only it didn't work out that way, because I was too vulnerable where you were concerned. To save myself, I brought forward my plans for going to Spain."

"But . . . but I thought that was because of Juanita."

Brett shook his head emphatically. "No, Juanita was irrelevant. She, Lynn, is the supreme example of the kind of female who had distorted my whole view of women. She's completely hard and calculating, and saw me as a potential second husband because she's bored with being a widow. In her case, though, it's not money and security she's after since she has a rich and indulgent father. It's purely a matter of status."

Lynn swallowed. "But . . . but I thought that you and Juanita . . . I mean, even Rafael said . . . "

"I took what was offered me." he acknowledged cynically. "Why shouldn't I?" Then, seeing Lynn flinch, he softened. "I promise you that Juanita has meant nothing to me since . . . well, for quite some time now. And when I tackled her yesterday and she actually admitted having maliciously damaged Don Fernando's portrait to get you into trouble, I really blew my top and told her I never wanted to see her again."

"You questioned Juanita about that?" Lynn was amazed. "But you wouldn't even listen when I hinted it might be her."

"I wouldn't listen because . . . because it was another stick to beat you with, Lynn. I'm utterly ashamed of how I behaved to you from start to finish. Looking back, I think I must have been a little out of my mind. But it's hardly surprising, when you consider the traumatic experience I'd been through in having you turn up at *Los Pámpanos* with Rafael. I felt like murder, Lynn, on that day."

"You looked capable of it! I could understand you being a bit annoyed with Rafael, and with me too, I suppose. But you seemed to be grossly over-reacting to the situation."

"You didn't know what the true situation was," he rejoined. "You only saw it as anger with Rafael for being so irresponsible, and with *you* for seeming to have your hooks into him as a good marriage prospect. But that's less than half the story! Before you turned up at *Los Pámpanos*, Lynn, there'd hardly been a minute when I'd not been thinking about you and wondering if perhaps I'd misjudged you. My heart and my head were at war over you, and in the end my heart won. I was just on the point of returning to England to see you again when you appeared from out of the blue — with my brother! God, in those first few moments I hated you both. And I felt a great blinding flash of fury against myself, because I'd let a woman undermine my defenses, when I'd always sworn it was something that would never happen. After I'd calmed down a bit, I decided that above all else I was going to see that you didn't get the chance to ruin Rafael's life. Because I was now fully armoured against you again — or so I thought — I considered I was in no danger by escorting you around myself. I never counted on your ability to steal your way into my heart."

"You mean at the picnic on the beach, when I hurt my ankle?" she ventured. "And that evening at Sanlúcar de Barrameda when we had dinner together?"

He nodded, his mouth set in grim lines. "And many other times! But although I fought desperately against the attraction you had for me, I couldn't get you out of my system. Each time I came across you and Rafael together I felt crazed with jealousy. The other evening, when I arrived back at *Los Pámpanos* late and saw you and Rafael out in the garden, and he was kissing your hands, it was all I could do not to rush out there and strangle you both."

"You don't understand, Brett. What you saw that night . . . well, Rafael finally accepted my word for it that there could never be anything between us, and he was saying goodbye."

"Is that really true? Oh God, if only I'd realised! It was seeing you like that which made me think up the plan for getting you on my boat for the night. I argued to myself that it would finally solve the problem of you and Rafael, because my brother would give up all thought of wanting to marry you when he knew that you'd spent a night with me. But there was another reason too, Lynn . . ."

"I suppose," she said, unable to conceal her bitterness, "you were confident by then that I'd never be able to hold out against you?"

"Yes."

It was a truth that Lynn couldn't deny, and she felt a rush of shame. Quickly she glanced away so that Brett shouldn't see the tears that had sprung to her eyes.

"You don't understand, Lynn darling," he went on gently. "I felt confident that if I were to get you away somewhere on our own, in the right romantic setting, I could force you to admit your true feelings for me — the feelings I knew you had always been fighting against. Some instinct told me that, once I had succeeded in making love to you, you would feel *committed* to me. That's what I was hoping for, I realise that now. I admit that my thinking was very muddled at the time — because another part of me was still insisting that you were just like every other woman. But at the same time, I'd always known deep down in my heart that you were different — the one woman I could love with all my heart and soul. The woman I wanted to spend the rest of my life with."

Lynn gasped incredulously, "You *love* me?"

"Oh yes, my darling, I love you. I love you quite desperately." Brett smiled in a rueful, puzzled sort of way. "I think I fell in love with you at first sight, that day I came across you sunbathing at the poolside at *La Casa Española*. It seemed like a dream, finding you there at my house, looking so lovely, so enchantingly lovely, and it did something to my heart. Only like a fool I stamped down my feelings of love and tenderness towards you and acted like I'd have acted with any other woman I found madly attractive and wanted to take to bed. As I said, I'd convinced myself that *all* women were only out for what they could get from a man, to trap him into marriage, so I refused to let myself believe that you were different. Oh my darling, how can I hope that you will ever find it in your heart to forgive me for the abominable way I've behaved . . . the vile way I've treated you?"

"I love you too, Brett!" It was as if her lips had formed the words of their own volition and she whispered them on a breath.

For long seconds he stared at her as though hardly daring to believe the evidence of his ears. Then, swiftly, he reached out and gathered her to him.

Lynn went into his arms joyously, forgetting all the days and weeks of torment and misery. She didn't stop to ask herself, in the wonder of finding herself loved by this man, how it was possible that Brett's kisses now, raining down upon her with such fervoured passion, could at the same time express all the sweet tenderness she had yearned for so desperately.

She clung to him as if suddenly afraid that he might escape, tangling her fingers into the crispness of his dark hair. As his desire mounted so her own rose to match it, until the fire of sweet torment threatened to engulf them. Then, a memory stirred within her that sent a wave of coldness shivering through her body.

Sensing her sudden withdrawal, Brett asked huskily, "Lynn, my darling, what is it? Do you not want me as I want you?"

Her eyes gave him his answer, her lustrous amber eyes that were huge with love and longing. But she whispered unhappily, "I am so afraid that if we . . . if I let you make love to me now, you will lose all respect for me."

Still holding her in a close embrace, Brett drew back a little and looked into her eyes with concern.

"My sweet, dearest one . . . what on earth gave you such an idea? As if *anything* could rob me of my respect for you."

Lynn formed the words with tense lips. "Rosa-María . . . she said that a woman must be steadfast in refusing a man if she is to keep his respect. And that, without respect, there will be no love for her in his heart."

Brett said slowly, "That may be true in the case of a passing fancy a man has for a girl. But I adore you, Lynn darling . . . I love you so desperately that I yearn to express what I feel in every possible way. Nothing will ever destroy my respect for you, you must believe that."

Lynn was angry with herself now, angry at her stupid blindness that would not let her understand the truth of Brett's feelings for her. She felt suddenly eager, impatient to prove her love for him, and she wound her arms round his neck and put her lips to his once more. But, to her dismay, Brett resisted and drew back.

"No, my darling," he said gently. "If I kissed you again at this moment, I don't think I could trust myself not to take possession of you here and now."

"I don't care," she said wildly. "I . . . I was being foolish. You mustn't think that I'd refuse you, Brett darling, not now or ever."

But still he held back, and the dark passion in his eyes gave way to the tenderness of a gentler love.

"We shall be married first," he insisted. "These things can be arranged at very short notice, and then we shall be man and wife. Lynn, my darling, do you want that as desperately as I do?"

"Oh Brett, you know I do."

"Let's talk about our honeymoon . . . you choose where, my love. What does it matter, as long as we're together. And afterwards, until we can find a proper home in London, we'll stay down in Sussex. Shall we keep *La Casa Española* as our place in the country, darling? Would you like that?"

"Oh yes," she breathed in a daze of delight.

The Spanish House, Lynn thought happily, where it had all begun.

## WITH SOMEBODY ELSE
### Theresa Charles

Rosamond sets off for Cornwall with Hugo to meet his family, blissfully unaware of the shocks in store for her.

## A SUMMER FOR STRANGERS
### Claire Hamilton

Because she had lost her job, her flat and she had no money, Tabitha agreed to pose as Adam's future wife although she believed the scheme to be deceitful and cruel.

## VILLA OF SINGING WATER
### Angela Petron

The disquieting incidents that occurred at the Vatican and the Colosseum did not trouble Jan at first, but then they became increasingly unpleasant and alarming.

## DOCTOR NAPIER'S NURSE
### Pauline Ash

When cousins Midge and Derry are entered as probationer nurses on the same day but at different hospitals they agree to exchange identities.

## A GIRL LIKE JULIE
### Louise Ellis

Caroline absolutely adored Hugh Barrington, but then Julie Crane came into their lives. Julie was the kind of girl who attracts men without even trying.

## COUNTRY DOCTOR
### Paula Lindsay

When Evan Richmond bought a practice in a remote country village he did not realise that a casual encounter would lead to the loss of his heart.

## ENCORE
### Helga Moray

Craig and Janet realise that their true happiness lies with each other, but it is only under traumatic circumstances that they can be reunited.

## NICOLETTE
### Ivy Preston

When Grant Alston came back into her life, Nicolette was faced with a dilemma. Should she follow the path of duty or the path of love?

## THE GOLDEN PUMA
### Margaret Way

Catherine's time was spent looking after her father's Queensland farm. But what life was there without David, who wasn't interested in her?

## HOSPITAL BY THE LAKE
### Anne Durham

Nurse Marguerite Ingleby was always ready to become personally involved with her patients, to the despair of Brian Field, the Senior Surgical Registrar, who loved her.

## VALLEY OF CONFLICT
### David Farrell

Isolated in a hostel in the French Alps, Ann Russell sees her fiancé being seduced by a young girl. Then comes the avalanche that imperils their lives.

## NURSE'S CHOICE
### Peggy Gaddis

A proposal of marriage from the incredibly handsome and wealthy Reagan was enough to upset any girl — and Brooke Martin was no exception.

## A DANGEROUS MAN
### Anne Goring

Photographer Polly Burton was on safari in Mombasa when she met enigmatic Leon Hammond. But unpredictability was the name of the game where Leon was concerned.

## PRECIOUS INHERITANCE
### Joan Moules

Karen's new life working for an authoress took her from Sussex to a foreign airstrip and a kidnapping; to a real life adventure as gripping as any in the books she typed.

## VISION OF LOVE
### Grace Richmond

When Kathy takes over the rundown country kennels she finds Alec Stinton, a local vet, very helpful. But their friendship arouses bitter jealousy and a tragedy seems inevitable.

## CRUSADING NURSE
### Jane Converse

It was handsome Dr. Corbett who opened Nurse Susan Leighton's eyes and who set her off on a lonely crusade against some powerful enemies and a shattering struggle against the man she loved.

## WILD ENCHANTMENT
### Christina Green

Rowan's agreeable new boss had a dream of creating a famous perfume using her precious Silverstar, but Rowan's plans were very different.

## DESERT ROMANCE
### Irene Ord

Sally agrees to take her sister Pam's place as La Chartreuse the dancer, but she finds out there is more to it than dyeing her hair red and looking like her sister.

## HEART OF ICE
### Marie Sidney

How was January to know that not only would the warmth of the Swiss people thaw out her frozen heart, but that she too would play her part in helping someone to live again?

## LUCKY IN LOVE
### Margaret Wood

Companion-secretary to wealthy gambler Laura Duxford, who lived in Monaco, seemed to Melanie a fabulous job. Especially as Melanie had already lost her heart to Laura's son, Julian.

## NURSE TO PRINCESS JASMINE
### Lilian Woodward

Nick's surgeon brother, Tom, performs an operation on an Arabian princess, and she invites Tom, Nick and his fiancé to Omander, where a web of deceit and intrigue closes about them.

## THE WAYWARD HEART
### Eileen Barry

Disaster-prone Katherine's nickname was "Kate Calamity", but her boss went too far with an outrageous proposal, which because of her latest disaster, she could not refuse.

## FOUR WEEKS IN WINTER
### Jane Donnelly

Tessa wasn't looking forward to meeting Paul Mellor again — she had made a fool of herself over him once before. But was Orme Jared's solution to her problem likely to be the right one?

## SURGERY BY THE SEA
### Sheila Douglas

Medical student Meg hadn't really wanted to go and work with a G.P. on the Welsh coast although the job had its compensations. But Owen Roberts was certainly not one of them!

## HEAVEN IS HIGH
### Anne Hampson

The new heir to the Manor of Marbeck had been found. But it was rather unfortunate that when he arrived unexpectedly he found an uninvited guest, complete with stetson and high boots.

## LOVE WILL COME
### Sarah Devon

June Baker's boss was not really her idea of her ideal man, but when she went from third typist to boss's secretary overnight she began to change her mind.

## ESCAPE TO ROMANCE
### Kay Winchester

Oliver and Jean first met on Swale Island. They were both trying to begin their lives afresh, but neither had bargained for complications from the past.

## CASTLE IN THE SUN
### Cora Mayne

Emma's invalid sister, Kym, needed a warm climate, and Emma jumped at the chance of a job on a Mediterranean island. But Emma soon finds that intrigues and hazards lurk on the sunlit isle.

## BEWARE OF LOVE
### Kay Winchester

Carol Brampton resumes her nursing career when her family is killed in a car accident. With Dr. Patrick Farrell she begins to pick up the pieces of her life, but is bitterly hurt when insinuations are made about her to Patrick.

## DARLING REBEL
### Sarah Devon

When Jason Farradale's secretary met with an accident, her glamorous stand-in was quite unable to deal with one problem in particular.